SEA FANGS

A full list of L. Ron Hubbard's
novellas and short stories is provided at the back.

*Dekalogy—a group of ten volumes

L. RON HUBBARD

SEA FANGS

GALAXY PRESS

Published by
Galaxy Press, LLC
7051 Hollywood Boulevard, Suite 200
Hollywood, CA 90028

Printed in the United States of America.

ISBN-10 1-59212-250-7
ISBN-13 978-1-59212-250-9

Library of Congress Control Number: 2007928126

CONTENTS

STORIES FROM PULP FICTION'S GOLDEN AGE

A ND it *was* a golden age.
The 1930s and 1940s were a vibrant, seminal time for a gigantic audience of eager readers, probably the largest per capita audience of readers in American history. The magazine racks were chock-full of publications with ragged trims, garish cover art, cheap brown pulp paper, low cover prices—and the most excitement you could hold in your hands.

"Pulp" magazines, named for their rough-cut, pulpwood paper, were a vehicle for more amazing tales than Scheherazade could have told in a million and one nights. Set apart from higher-class "slick" magazines, printed on fancy glossy paper with quality artwork and superior production values, the pulps were for the "rest of us," adventure story after adventure story for people who liked to *read*. Pulp fiction authors were no-holds-barred entertainers—real storytellers. They were more interested in a thrilling plot twist, a horrific villain or a white-knuckle adventure than they were in lavish prose or convoluted metaphors.

The sheer volume of tales released during this wondrous golden age remains unmatched in any other period of literary history—hundreds of thousands of published stories in over nine hundred different magazines. Some titles lasted only an issue or two; many magazines succumbed to paper shortages during World War II, while others endured for decades yet. Pulp fiction remains as a treasure trove of stories you can read, stories you can love, stories you can remember. The stories were driven by plot and character, with grand heroes, terrible villains, beautiful damsels (often in distress), diabolical plots, amazing places, breathless romances. The readers wanted to be taken beyond the mundane, to live adventures far removed from their ordinary lives—and the pulps rarely failed to deliver.

In that regard, pulp fiction stands in the tradition of all memorable literature. For as history has shown, good stories are much more than fancy prose. William Shakespeare, Charles Dickens, Jules Verne, Alexandre Dumas—many of the greatest literary figures wrote their fiction for the readers, not simply literary colleagues and academic admirers. And writers for pulp magazines were no exception. These publications reached an audience that dwarfed the circulations of today's short story magazines. Issues of the pulps were scooped up and read by over thirty million avid readers each month.

Because pulp fiction writers were often paid no more than a cent a word, they had to become prolific or starve. They also had to write aggressively. As Richard Kyle, publisher and editor of *Argosy,* the first and most long-lived of the pulps, so pointedly explained: "The pulp magazine writers, the best of them, worked for markets that did not write for critics or attempt to satisfy timid advertisers. Not having to answer to anyone other than their readers, they wrote about human beings on the edges of the unknown, in those new lands the future would explore. They wrote for what we would become, not for what we had already been."

Some of the more lasting names that graced the pulps include H. P. Lovecraft, Edgar Rice Burroughs, Robert E. Howard, Max Brand, Louis L'Amour, Elmore Leonard, Dashiell Hammett, Raymond Chandler, Erle Stanley Gardner, John D. MacDonald, Ray Bradbury, Isaac Asimov, Robert Heinlein—and, of course, L. Ron Hubbard.

In a word, he was among the most prolific and popular writers of the era. He was also the most enduring—hence this series—and certainly among the most legendary. It all began only months after he first tried his hand at fiction, with L. Ron Hubbard tales appearing in *Thrilling Adventures, Argosy, Five-Novels Monthly, Detective Fiction Weekly, Top-Notch, Texas Ranger, War Birds, Western Stories,* even *Romantic Range.* He could write on any subject, in any genre, from jungle explorers to deep-sea divers, from G-men and gangsters, cowboys and flying aces to mountain climbers, hard-boiled detectives and spies. But he really began to shine when he turned his talent to science fiction and fantasy of which he authored nearly fifty novels or novelettes to forever change the shape of those genres.

Following in the tradition of such famed authors as Herman Melville, Mark Twain, Jack London and Ernest Hemingway, Ron Hubbard actually lived adventures that his own characters would have admired—as an ethnologist among primitive tribes, as prospector and engineer in hostile climes, as a captain of vessels on four oceans. He even wrote a series of articles for *Argosy,* called "Hell Job," in which he lived and told of the most dangerous professions a man could put his hand to.

Finally, and just for good measure, he was also an accomplished photographer, artist, filmmaker, musician and educator. But he was first and foremost a *writer,* and that's the L. Ron Hubbard we come to know through the pages of this volume.

This library of Stories from the Golden Age presents the best of L. Ron Hubbard's fiction from the heyday of storytelling, the Golden Age of the pulp magazines. In these eighty volumes, readers are treated to a full banquet of 153 stories, a kaleidoscope of tales representing every imaginable genre: science fiction, fantasy, western, mystery, thriller, horror, even romance—action of all kinds and in all places.

Because the pulps themselves were printed on such inexpensive paper with high acid content, issues were not meant to endure. As the years go by, the original issues of every pulp from *Argosy* through *Zeppelin Stories* continue crumbling into brittle, brown dust. This library preserves the L. Ron Hubbard tales from that era, presented with a distinctive look that brings back the nostalgic flavor of those times.

L. Ron Hubbard's Stories from the Golden Age has something for every taste, every reader. These tales will return you to a time when fiction was good clean entertainment and the most fun a kid could have on a rainy afternoon or the best thing an adult could enjoy after a long day at work.

Pick up a volume, and remember what reading is supposed to be all about. Remember curling up with a *great story*.

—Kevin J. Anderson

KEVIN J. ANDERSON *is the author of more than ninety critically acclaimed works of speculative fiction, including The Saga of Seven Suns, the continuation of the Dune Chronicles with Brian Herbert, and his* New York Times *bestselling novelization of L. Ron Hubbard's* Ai! Pedrito!

SEA FANGS

CHAPTER ONE

THE STRICKEN YACHT

THE teeth of the hurricane shook the plunging *Bonito* from stem to stern each time the dripping bows uprooted the gray, hurtling seas. From the bridge it was almost impossible to view the white yacht's forward house, and the intensity of the spray not only blinded the ports of the flying bridge, but had already smashed out two heavy panes of glass.

Through these two openings the hurricane threw lashing coils of wind and water which swirled about the slickered body of the tall helmsman. The man's steel-blue eyes were smarted by the whip of the salt water, and he squinted to see the binnacle more clearly. Although the compass was crashing backward and forward as though spun by a mighty hand, and the wheel was a live thing that fought the confining long fingers with the fury and strength of a thing gone mad, the helmsman braced his strong shoulders against the lash of the sea and tried to keep the once-trim *Bonito* close into the blast.

To the captain, huddled in a protected wing of the bridge, the helmsman was a mere waterfront loafer who had signed on at New York. And to the man at the wheel the captain was a paid servant of fabulously rich people. But together they were two human beings who fought the destruction of the screaming wind oblivious of the panic-stricken passengers below decks, intent only upon holding out until this blow should pass.

The captain stepped up beside the binnacle, clutching at it for support.

"Hold her into it!" he yelled above the roar of the storm. "She's swinging off!"

He snatched the wheel away from the sailor and tried to pull it over a spoke. But the wheel lashed back once, and then spun madly in the opposite direction. The sailor risked bruised hands and stopped it, brought his back against it, swung it up, up, up, until the bow was once more taking the coming sea full on the nose.

"Get the hell back into the wing!" cried the sailor. "Are you trying to wreck us?"

The captain's fists clenched for an instant, and then an unexpectedly heavy sea made him clutch at the binnacle again. He crept back to the protected wing.

Bob Sherman, the sailor, wrested his eyes from the compass long enough to frown in the direction of the wing. Looking back at the spinning disk he frowned again. Old Herbert Marmion, owner of the *Bonito,* might know something of the art of making money, but he was certainly short on judging men. This Captain Stoddard was all right when it came to officiating at pink teas, but he was a dead loss where seamanship was concerned.

Sherman had the papers of a master mariner down in his sea bag, but he was not going to unfold his hand just yet. It was not his business if the *Bonito* sprung every rivet in her trim hull. Still, he had shown Stoddard that dropping barometer, had even explained what a hurricane meant down here off the treacherous coast of Venezuela. And Captain Stoddard had told him to finish painting the stack and leave seamanship to someone who understood it.

The caking salt on Sherman's cheeks had long ago begun to eat into his bronze skin, and the spray had found its stinging way down inside the slicker, making his clothes cling to his hard body. But there was something in this fight with the hurricane that avenged all the wrongs the sea had done him in the past three years. In reality, of course, the misdeeds lay at the door of Herbert Marmion and a certain outfit of outlaw smugglers and revolutionists who held sway over their small islands a few miles out from the Gulf of Venezuela. But the sea's brute force, brought to him through the broken ports, was ample challenge to his tremendous strength, and Bob Sherman fought on.

The chief officer, a silky man named Hardesty, came out of a passageway and tapped Sherman on the shoulder. "You've had it an hour!" he yelled. He motioned two sailors out of the passage and to the wheel.

The two sailors laid trembling, and immediately wet, hands upon that terrible wheel, and looked up at Sherman. He released the wheel as though the action was distasteful to him.

"The stewards," cried the chief officer, "are all in their bunks. Will you go below and lend a hand?"

Sherman nodded assent and stooped to enter the open door. Bracing himself against the sides of the passageway, he worked his way aft. At the top of a companionway he pulled his sou'wester from his hair and whipped the streams of water away from his coat. Then he pulled the oilskin hat over his right eye and dropped to the lower deck.

He found himself in the main salon and paused for a moment to stare around at the havoc the storm had caused. Heavy chairs lay broken on their sides. The grand piano had lost all but one of its legs. Drapes were tangled about mahogany tables, and rugs were snarled bits of color on the water-soaked deck.

Sherman held to a rail for support and stood there with a grim smile on his face. It gave him something like pleasure to see the belongings of the Marmions so drastically ruined. He glanced toward the row of doors which designated the owner's quarters and smiled again. All the Marmions and their friends were within those doors, seasick, stricken with fear. But as he looked one of the doors swung back, and Sherman found himself looking at Marmion's daughter.

She was black-haired and dark-eyed. Her face was drawn with worry, but when she saw him she smiled and picked her way across the heaving deck.

"You're one of the sailors, aren't you?" she said.

He looked down at her and nodded, without smiling.

"Please. I need some help terribly. Dad's lying on the floor of his cabin and I can't get him back into his bunk." She started back across the salon, clinging to upset chairs to steady herself against the pitch and roll of the *Bonito*.

Sherman followed her, scorning handholds. He saw her step into the first cabin and he looked in through the door.

Herbert Marmion lay sprawled miserably on the littered rug. Sherman stepped through and encircled the man's body with strong arms. Without seeming effort, he picked the man up and shoved him into the bunk. The man lay there, moaning.

Suddenly the fat-rimmed eyes started wide and the soft, plump hands clawed at Bob's slicker.

"Are we going to sink?"

"How should I know? Ask that two-for-a-nickel captain of yours!" Sherman swung around and went back into the passageway, Herbert Marmion's panicky cries following him.

The girl followed Sherman out and closed the door. She looked up at the sailor, a troubled expression in her eyes. She tugged at his arm. Bringing her mouth close to his ear, she said, "Who are you?"

"You wouldn't be interested." Sherman stared hard at her for a moment. "Who's next?" he said abruptly.

The girl frowned and led down the passageway to a pantry. She stepped in, making her way around broken dishes and dented pans. Picking up a copper coffeepot, she made a helpless gesture in the direction of the door. Sherman entered and looked about. He saw a small oil stove and a water tappet. Pointing to a can of coffee lashed on the shelf, he applied a match to the stove and stood back, watching the blue flame lick around the wick.

The girl handed him the filled pot. Bob lashed two towels around the handle and spout, and tied it on the stove. He glanced back and saw that the girl had seated herself on a built-in table and was quietly considering him. He noted with indifference that she was beautiful. Her hair was swept

7

back from her forehead and was glisteningly jet-black. Her eyes were almost as dark as her hair. Yes, Sherman thought, she showed more beauty and breeding than he would have expected in a Marmion.

The coffee was boiling, and Sherman wrapped the towels around it and picked it up. The girl took several heavy cups from the debris on the floor and led the way back up the passage. But no one wanted coffee—neither the girl's father and mother, nor Percy Gilman, her fiancé, nor any of the Marmions' friends.

The girl and Sherman went back to the pantry. He set the coffee pot in a corner where the contents wouldn't spill, and, at the girl's invitation, sat down on the built-in table. Then he saw that a ventilator above was letting spray down upon them and he closed it. He kicked the pantry doors shut and found that he had blotted out the sound of the raging hurricane. The girl poured out two cups of coffee, and they sat down on the table again.

The girl was staring across the narrow pantry at a fragment of china, nursing the warmth of the cup in her two slender hands.

"I don't blame you for being a swashbuckler, Bob."

Sherman started and spilled some of his coffee.

"How did you know my name?"

The girl smiled.

CHAPTER TWO

LOST IDENTITY

S HE spoke musingly. "Of course you wouldn't remember. It was at a Crescent Yacht Club dance about five years ago. You were there fresh from South America, and your yacht, the *Seafarer*, was anchored out in the stream. She was romantic, that yacht. I was in my last year of college—just one of two dozen such girls." She smiled suddenly. "But you did give me a nice smile, Bob!"

He regarded her with screened eyes. It was very possible, for in those days life had been a constant round of such dances.

"I'm afraid I don't remember," he said. "Not even your first name."

"Phyllis. That's the first name. Phyllis. You don't like the last, which is Marmion. I can't say that I blame you, at that. Dad is rather hard when it comes to business deals. Didn't you ever recover a dime out of your Venezuelan oil fields?"

Sherman drained the last of his coffee. He had signed on as John Smith so that they would not uncover his real name on the ship's articles. He had counted on remaining on the bridge and in the fo'c's'le, that they might not see him. Still, he hadn't even suspected that Marmion knew him on sight. To Marmion, Robert Sherman had been a name that suddenly ceased to be signed on Venezuelan dividend checks.

9

The girl drained her cup, and brought a damp packet of cigarettes from her almost transparent slicker. She offered him one, and he took it. Lighting up, they blew smoke across the narrow pantry. If it had not been for the pitching and rolling they would have forgotten all about the hurricane.

Phyllis Marmion spoke again. "Tell me about yourself."

"You wouldn't be interested."

"Oh, please," Phyllis protested. "Don't take that attitude!"

"Well, at least it will while away the time." Sherman took a long drag and blew smoke toward the bulkhead. "I landed in New York a couple months ago, down and out. Didn't know where I could get a meal. All the fine friends I had a few years ago sniffed politely. Oh, yes, to them I was just a blond beggar, without connections or funds. They didn't have time for me. They'd rather throw parties for your father."

"Don't say that," the girl protested. "Dad isn't so bad, once you know him."

"Then I hope I'll get to know him soon." Sherman smiled again. "Do you want to hear a story that couldn't be true?"

"I'd love it," Phyllis assured him.

"All right." Sherman's voice was suddenly whimsical.

"Once upon a time there was a little boy who thought he was hot stuff, and his name was Bob Sherman. Are you sure you want to hear this?"

"Of course!"

"Well, this little boy promoted three thousand acres of oil land in a country where the sun is hot and the natives lazy and the politicians crooked. And he had more money than he could ever possibly spend. So he bought himself a yacht and named her the *Seafarer*." Sherman poured himself another cup of coffee, and went on.

"He was very optimistic. He thought he owned all Seven Seas and had a lease on the continents. But he didn't. No, he didn't." He smiled at Phyllis and drank his coffee. She had time to notice that he was more ruggedly handsome than he had been five years before.

"A certain person named Marmion had those leases and deeds all the time." Sherman's eyes became steely. "This Marmion paid certain political leaders a certain sum of money to have those fields condemned for government use. The fields were condemned after Sherman had stopped two machine-gun slugs and lost four men and his foreman.

Phyllis' eyes narrowed. "Bob! Dad wouldn't do a thing like that!"

"No, he wouldn't—but he did. And those fields were leased to him for a period of one hundred years, ten percent of the gross to the government." Sherman drew another cigarette from the girl's pack, and looked up. "Please don't get angry, Miss Marmion."

But Phyllis Marmion's eyes held nothing but sympathy for the blond giant seated beside her.

He resumed his story. "Anyway, Bob Sherman was broke. But he still had his yacht, the *Seafarer,* and he set out from Cartagena to see what he could do about things. Somebody told him that there was a hotbed of revolutionists and smugglers on a small island in the sea off the Gulf of Venezuela. Bob Sherman suddenly conceived a rash idea. He was going to start himself a revolution, unseat the president of Venezuela, and get that oil land back again. So he went out to find the island stronghold—and there he arrived, amid a flash of spray."

Phyllis waited for a long time for the rest of the story. She watched the steel blue eyes intently. "Go on. Don't keep me in suspense. Did you start the revolution?"

Sherman laughed. "No. I'd suddenly lost my lease on the continents. So Sherman sailed into a cove with wide open eyes and talked with some of the ugliest specimens of humanity now extant. They have an old Spanish fort and a town of stucco houses. They've even a couple of field pieces out on the point, for a guard. Those fellows use revolution to hide their real activities. You might call them pirates.

"To make a long story brief, they took the *Seafarer* and placed Bob Sherman in a deep and exceedingly dirty dungeon in the fort. Then they made him into a sort of maid of all work. He was there for eighteen months."

"Really?" Phyllis cried. "How on earth did you escape?"

"Oh, a pistol was lying handy one day and I used it on one of the guards. I took a small boat out of the harbor at night and drifted around in the steamer lane until I was picked up. After that, I went to New York and signed on a yacht named the *Bonito*, under the name of John Smith. I intended to find out all I could about that deal by being close to Mr. Marmion. But—instead—I meet his very attractive daughter."

Phyllis smiled. She had forgotten about the hurricane and everything else in the world but Bob Sherman.

He got up from the table and looked at the closed pantry

door. Phyllis thrust out an impulsive hand. Sherman looked down at its white slimness and then closed his long, tanned fingers over it. For a moment he clasped it. Then he smiled at Phyllis, laid a quick kiss in the palm of her hand, and strode out, leaving the girl staring at the spot his lips had touched.

With the roar of the hurricane again in his ears, but feeling somehow better about the world in general, Sherman made his way back to the flying bridge. He buckled down the sou'wester and stepped to the wet decks and felt once more the sting of that salt spray against his face. He looked at the wing where he had seen the captain last, but found it empty. Planting his feet against the swoop of the deck, he made his way to the chart room.

The captain and the chief officer were spilling water on the face of a hydrographic chart, and Captain Stoddard was running the end of a compass across his teeth. Both men stared hard at Sherman as he came up to the desk and leaned against it.

"What the hell are you doing in here?" the captain shouted.

Sherman stared down with a steady eye, and then pointed to the chart.

"Are you supposed to be where you've got that blue cross?" he said.

The chief officer frowned, then nodded.

Sherman picked up a blue pencil and made another cross, one much larger than the first. His cross showed their position to be much farther west, and only a few miles off the coast of Venezuela. "This wind is blowing you backwards at least ten knots."

13

"How do you know?" Stoddard's tone was belligerent. "Because I've been in more hurricanes off this coast than you've ever read about. There's a current in here that runs strong to the west when there's a high wind. They haven't got it in the *Coast Pilot*s. You'll either rig up a sea anchor to· hold her, or you'll run right into Point Gallinas."

The captain's face went a sickly gray, and he stared down at the chart, hypnotized by Sherman's cross. Then he looked at the mate with troubled, questioning eyes.

"I don't know," the chief officer snapped. "This is my first time in these waters. You'd better take the sailor's word for it."

Stoddard considered the chart for a long moment, obviously unsure of his own judgment. A hurricane had never before confronted him. Then he brightened, picked up the blue pencil.

"Look!" He was excited. "We can head into the Gulf of Venezuela." He drew a line from Sherman's cross into the Gulf.

But Bob Sherman saw that the line came close to a black, unnamed pinpoint which called attention to an island.

"No!" he said. "Rig the anchor. Don't go in there."

But the captain had regained something of his sense of command, and while he allowed Sherman's cross to stay on the face of the chart, he refused to listen to further suggestions.

"Who the hell's captain of this ship, anyway?" he said at last.

Sherman started to speak, then changed his mind. After all, the chances were ten to one against their coming within miles of that unnamed speck of land. He stepped out the door, and found that he was suddenly weary.

14

The hurricane had lasted since midnight, and it was now late in the afternoon, although the grayness of the skies blended with the hurtling ranges of waves that smashed into the *Bonito*. And for all those hours, Sherman had been on his feet, over half the time at the wheel, doing two men's work.

At the jerking wheel, the two men held feverishly to the wet, slippery spokes. Each time the *Bonito* sank her nose into an oncoming wave, she stayed there a moment, shuddering, while the engines below threshed, the props out of water. And when the stem came down again, treacherous cross waves bit at the rudder, causing the wheel to swing and writhe.

The two sailors gripped the wheel and tried to keep the compass disc steady. One of them was a boy not yet twenty, and the strain of his efforts showed grimly in his face. He was unwilling to give up, but obviously unable to go on with the fight.

Sherman stepped between them and took the helm. With a glance of thanks, the two stepped back, beating their numbed hands together to restore circulation. Sherman's seasoned muscles and trained hands bent to the task, and he braced his long, hard body against the crashing shocks of the lashing rudder. He was tired, but he was used to the work, and he discovered that a warm glow had crept up inside of him. He traced this sudden feeling of well-being, and the trail went back to the built-in table in the pantry below.

Two sailors came up to relieve him, and the chief officer drew Sherman into the wing.

"I want a sounding," the chief officer said. "Think you can

get one? The Lucas reel on the stern is busted, and you'll have to take it off the fo'c's'le."

Sherman smiled faintly. He knew by the look in the chief officer's eyes that he was afraid to go forward and take that sounding himself.

"All right. Cut down the headway and get me a telephone to plug in up there."

The mate looked relieved and went into the chart room for an extension field telephone.

Sherman placed the instrument under his slicker and went forward. Waves were crashing over the fo'c's'le head, and water was knee-deep in the well deck. Going was hard, for most of the lifelines, which had been rigged up at the beginning of the storm, were now treacherous tangles on the planking.

He huddled in the lee of the fo'c's'le for a moment, waiting for a wave to break. Then he drew a long breath and swung up the ladder.

The tremendous force of the wind threatened to blast him away from the ship, and the spray made sight almost impossible, but he made his way from handhold to handhold, until the reel of the Lucas sounding device was located. He found a plug in the deck for the field telephone and snapped it in, hoping that the water would not short it.

Waves beat him relentlessly and he had to lean heavily into the wind to swing out the boom and rig the wires. He hitched the telephone under him and lay at full length on the slippery deck, holding to the base of the reel. Then he found the release and let it go. Wire began to sing out of the reel, along the boom and into the sea. He couldn't hear the whine, but he could feel the vibration of the reel. He gave the brake a few turns, taking up on the reel as the wire paid out.

Between mouthfuls of salt water he yelled into the telephone. "Slack off a point! Another point! One more! Cut down the headway!"

From the change in pitching, he could tell that the helmsmen were following his orders, and from the sudden violent rolls, he knew that the *Bonito* was slowing up.

The reel ceased to spin, and he read the mark.

"One hundred and ten fathom!" Repeating this several times, he brought the wire back up. Then he let it out again. "One hundred and fifteen fathom!" A third sounding. "One hundred and twelve fathom!"

Voices mumbled to him in the receiver, but his head was half submerged and he could not understand. Confident that his data had been sufficient for Captain Stoddard to accurately place the *Bonito* in the mouth of the Gulf of Venezuela, Sherman reeled in the wire and prepared to go aft.

He made his way to the top of the ladder that led down to the well deck, bracing himself against the repeated shocks of breaking waves and rushing wind. His hand caught at the bitt, which showed black below green water.

For a long, agonizing moment he knew that he had missed his hold. He felt himself plunging down, carried along in a fury of water. He knew that he would be lucky to land on deck in any condition, for an expanse of gray sea licked hungrily at him. He was blinded, choked. He felt himself tumbling over and over in frothy space. Something struck at him cruelly, and he lost consciousness.

17

CHAPTER THREE

DEATH ISLAND

I T was night when Bob Sherman found that he was staring up at a stained blue ceiling. He could tell that it was night because the round porthole was dark and a single bulb glowed above him. He found that his body was encased in damp sheets, and that it hurt him when he tried to move. Then he saw that he was not in the fo'c's'le where he belonged, and his eyes darted about the room.

Phyllis Marmion was seated beside him.

"Hello, old-timer," she said.

He looked at her for a full minute, noting that her face was pale from weariness.

"I got hurt, didn't I? Why did you bring me in here?" he said.

The girl pulled the sheets up around his chin and smiled. "Yes, you're hurt. They brought you back from the well deck half drowned. As for bringing you in here, I wanted a good chance to look at your face."

Sherman grinned, and then glanced toward the port, making a discovery. "Why, it's stopped blowing!"

"Yes, it's stopped. Captain Stoddard found the lee of a small island, and he didn't waste any time dropping the hook."

Leaning back, Sherman found that the pillow was almost as soft as the girl's hands. He lay inert, his eyes on Phyllis Marmion's face. Then a fearful thought clouded his eyes.

19

"But, say! What's the name of this island?" he said, sharply.

Phyllis shrugged. "Don't bother your head about that. It hasn't any name, from what I can find out. It's just a piece of land that happened to be convenient."

"Will you send for Stoddard?" Sherman propped himself up on an elbow and gave her a pleading look. "Tell him it's important."

Phyllis considered the request thoughtfully. "He's probably turned in by now, but if you want to speak to him, all right." She had not considered it odd that she should summon a captain at the request of a sailor.

Fifteen minutes later, Stoddard pounded on the door of the cabin and entered. He was sodden from lack of sleep, but when he saw Sherman lying at ease in the cabin, he scowled.

"Taking it easy, aren't you, sailor?" he said harshly.

Phyllis intervened, as Sherman started to speak. "You'll please be civil in my presence, Captain Stoddard. If he had not given you those soundings you never would have been able to find this island for protection. Now go ahead, Bob."

Bob lost no time. "Captain, where does your chart show this island to be?"

Stoddard gave the girl a wrathful glance, then looked back at Bob. "Just off the mouth of the Gulf of Venezuela, mister. Could I have it moved for you?"

"Belay the sarcasm, Stoddard—this is serious." Sherman drew a long breath, and plunged on. "You're probably just off *la isla de la muerte,* the Island of Death. You'd better get under weigh as soon as you can."

The captain smiled scornfully. "I suppose you think I'm going out into that blow again, just to please a sailor's whim!"

He turned to go, but Phyllis stopped him.

"What does that mean, Bob?" she said.

"Just this." Sherman's eyes were cold as steel. "The Island of Death is the headquarters of Venezuelan revolutionists, smugglers. Pirates, if you like. I just got out of there after an eighteen months' stay, and I don't intend to let Captain Stoddard's bullheadedness put us ashore and into the hands of those murderers. Hurricane or typhoon, Captain, you're going to get this ship out of here in ten minutes. Otherwise, you'll have blood on your hands, and worse!"

Stoddard's lip curled in disbelief. "What's the game, mister? This yacht is going to stay right where she is until I can repair her bow plates and get some of this clutter off the decks. An hour after your little foray forward, we broke a reduction gear. Now please, for the sake of the ladies aboard, snap out of it!" The captain shook off Phyllis' detaining fingers, and slammed the door behind him.

"Nice fellow," Phyllis said drily.

"Swell! There's only one thing to do, and that's to call your father in here and have him order Stoddard to weigh anchor."

Phyllis smiled wearily. "Dad's still in his bunk. He couldn't say two consecutive words if his life depended upon it. Bob, do you really think that's Death Island out there?"

Sherman shrugged. "It would be just like the sea to bring me back where I least want to return. You can do this, Miss

21

Marmion—collect three or four guns. There should be some aboard."

"Right you are. I'll do my best."

Sherman listened to her light footfalls receding down the passage. Two thoughts lay in his tired mind—that it was awful to be lying here helpless within a stone's throw of Death Island, and that Phyllis Marmion had the power to make him feel happy or wretched at will.

Phyllis returned with a riot gun and two automatic pistols. She laid these on the floor beside his bed, and then pulled boxes and bandoliers of ammunition from her pockets.

"Now," she said, "we can hold out for a little while, can't we?"

He noticed that she didn't appear at all worried by the prospects he had convinced her they faced.

"Probably so," he said. "It's certain that they won't come out until this sea quiets down enough for small boats."

Phyllis dropped some white tablets into a glass of water and handed it to him.

"You'll feel better, if you drink this," she said.

Sherman drained the glass and smiled.

She pulled the sheets up around his throat again and smoothed them out along the bed. Then she looked down at him intently.

"Feel better?"

He frowned a little. "I'm starting to feel sleepy. What did you give me?"

She watched until his eyelids became heavy. "You need a few hours' sleep, Bob. I thought I'd better give them to you while I could." She smoothed out his tumbled hair and caressed his forehead lightly with her fingers. Then she bent down quickly and kissed his mouth.

Bob's eyes shot wide a moment, then closed. "Lord!" he murmured happily. "You're swell—Phyllis." He drew a heavy breath and then was asleep.

An hour before dawn he awoke. His body had stopped aching and his head was clear. He turned over and faced the cabin.

Sitting with her arm along the edge of his bunk and her black hair falling down on the sheets, Phyllis Marmion was sound asleep.

Sherman raised up cautiously and slid down to the bottom of the berth. Silently he stepped to the floor. He placed his arms about the sleeping girl and lifted her softly into the bunk. She sighed and nestled down against him as he placed her head on the pillow.

He stood back, looking at her, then bent and kissed her tenderly.

Thrusting one of the pistols into his belt, he placed the other beside Phyllis. Then cradling the riot gun in the crook of his arm, he stepped out, closing the cabin door quietly behind him.

The keen tang of salt water met him as he went out to the deck. He saw gear tangled everywhere. The lifeboats were stove in, ports were broken, halyards lay in sodden, gray coils against the brown, wet planking. In the gray half-light of the coming dawn, the *Bonito* appeared to be irrevocably wrecked, but Sherman knew that a few hours' work would replace the gear and undo much of the damage.

Swinging lazily on her chains, the *Bonito* was pointed in toward a headland which loomed spectrally out of the mist. Sherman needed but one glance to know that he was again looking at *la isla de la muerte*. She looked like death now, with those gray wisps of vapor eddying about her, for she was silhouetted black against the graying east.

He shifted the riot gun with a restless jerk of his wrist. He almost saw, even now, mestizos and Spaniards swinging up over the rail. He knew that it was only a question of time before speedboats, armed with machine guns, would swing away from that black shoreline to race toward the *Bonito*.

Running up the bridge ladder, he made his way to the captain's cabin. He went in without knocking, and found Stoddard sitting on the bunk in his underwear. Before he could speak, the captain grinned.

With a sneer in his voice, the captain said, "Quite easy to get, the little Marmion, eh, sailor?"

Rage flamed in Sherman's eyes. He dropped the riot gun to the rug and was beside Stoddard in two strides.

Before the captain could make an outcry, or even begin to realize what was about to happen to him, he felt himself swung up from the berth, felt himself catapult through the air and crash against his desk. He lay still.

Sherman stood over him, quivering with rage. He knew what he had done, and he knew that it was a court offense to strike down a captain on the high seas, but the captain's insult to Phyllis had been too much.

A voice in the open door made Sherman whirl. It was the chief officer.

"You're under arrest, sailor. Come with me."

Sherman smiled faintly. "If you want me to go with you, step in and take me."

The chief officer blinked and looked at the hard, muscular body before him. He stammered a moment, feeling for words. The suggestion of battle with the blond giant unnerved him.

Sherman cut in on his thoughts. "He slurred Miss Marmion, but that's neither here nor elsewhere. We're about to be attacked from shore. Go round up the crew and get plenty of guns and ammunition."

The unnerved mate stared open-mouthed, then, in spite of himself, jerked his hand to the peak of his cap. "Yes, sir." He disappeared down the passageway, too startled to question the sailor's statement.

Including the black gang, there were twelve in the crew and six in the steward's department. Sherman and the chief officer lined them up on the well deck.

"Men," Sherman began, "the chief officer tells me that this ship is unable to get under weigh until certain repairs are made to the engine." The chief officer nodded assent. "Two men of the black gang will go below immediately with the chief engineer and try to repair that damage without delay." He pointed to the rifles and pistols the first mate had collected. "The rest of you will arm yourselves with these and

25

station yourselves along the rail. Don't show yourselves until you hear a whistle from the bridge. Understand?"

The sailors and stewards looked at one another restively. Then they looked back at the tall sailor who commanded them with such assurance. All question went out of their faces and they moved to do his bidding. The black gang's designated members went below. The others picked up rifles and pistols.

Sherman caught at the cook's arm. "Go aft and make coffee and sandwiches."

The chief engineer, a dried-up Scot, approached the mate.

"What's the meaning of this? Where's Stoddard, and who's in command around here, anyway?"

The chief mate started to speak, but Sherman stepped up in front of the chief engineer.

"This is irregular, I know," Sherman said, "but Stoddard is ill. That is *la isla de la muerte* off there. I know the place only too well. If you can get that reduction gear patched up in a hurry, we'll be able to get out of danger. But while we're here, attack is imminent. You will please go below and get to work on the gear."

The Scot gazed at the steely eyes of the sailor perplexedly. Suddenly he smiled.

"All right, sir. I'll see what I can do."

Sherman looked around him. The second mate, a gangly youth, had been leaning up against the forward mast. But now he moved quickly to the diminished pile of rifles. He selected one, and busily worked the bolt back and forth.

The chief officer tugged at his tailored, but rumpled collar.

"Lordy, sailor, I couldn't have done that. Who are you, anyway?"

"You wouldn't be interested. I'm going aft to see what I can do in the cabins." Sherman swung away abruptly and went up the ladder that led to a passage off the main salon.

CHAPTER FOUR

HUMAN WRECKAGE

IN the half-light of dawn, the main salon looked even more wrecked than it had the afternoon before. Sherman entered the cabin of Mr. Marmion, and tugged at the fleshy body.

"Go away!" came a gruff voice. "I'm sick! Go away!"

Sherman went on down the passageway to Edward Bushby's door. He found Bushby seated on a transom berth staring down at the carpet.

"I want you to go forward," Sherman said.

Bushby's voice was irritated. "And who the devil are you?"

"It doesn't matter." Sherman pulled the pale-faced promoter to his feet. "We'll have a fight on our hands in another hour. Get forward."

Bushby inched out the door.

"Mr. Marmion and Captain Stoddard are going to hear about this," he muttered.

Young Percy Gilman lay in a tangle of sheets in his bunk, and when Sherman came up beside him he made as if to push the sailor away.

"Get out of here!" he whined. "You wouldn't pull at me that way if you knew I might die any minute."

Sherman smiled mirthlessly. "Get below and forward, son. If you've ever smelled powder smoke, you'll be right at home in about an hour."

29

Sherman avoided Phyllis' cabin, and knew that there was little use in troubling either Mrs. Marmion or her friends. They would find out the truth only too soon.

Back on the flying bridge, he found that the chief officer had placed the captain in his bunk and was now busily sweeping the shoreline with a pair of field glasses.

"As soon as the mist clears," Sherman said, "you'll be able to see the waterfront of the town. We're lying just off it. There's two stone quays and a cluster of stucco buildings. An old Spanish fort is up above them on a hill. There are two field pieces out here on this point." He took the other's glasses. "Look to the right of that peak and you'll see the quays. Do you think we can drift out a little further if we weigh anchor?"

"Wouldn't try it, if I were you. There are some nasty looking rocks to stern." He swept the glasses in a wide arc. "Yes, I see a building. Look, what's that out there?" He thrust the glasses toward Sherman.

He could see it with his naked eye. "Speedboat!"

He went into the captain's cabin and picked the riot gun off the floor. Coming back to the flying bridge, he rammed a long clip into the magazine with a determined click. The fresh morning breeze rippled his tattered and dirty white pants and beat the collar of his white jacket against his broad shoulders. As he waited for the oncoming speedboat, his mouth drew into a hard gash across his lean face.

The speedboat lashed by the port side of the *Bonito* and spun about to come up along the starboard. There were six men in the cockpit—five ugly, dirty mestizos, and one tall, falcon-faced Spaniard. Two of the men gripped hungrily on the belt and handle of the snub-nosed machine gun in the bow.

Hola!" cried the tall one in the stern. "You will please do me the favor of coming ashore immediately!"

Sherman watched the speedboat go into reverse and then hang directly under the wing of the bridge. His Spanish crackled.

"I give you three minutes to go out of range of the guns. Go, pigs, while you are still able!"

"Hah!" yelled the tall one angrily. "It is you again!" He whirled to the machine gunners, and his voice snapped. The speedboat churned water and darted away.

The two gunners spun their weapon on the tripod and angled the fat muzzle at the bridge. Sherman saw it spit flame, heard the whine of striking lead, saw the mate reel back. Up came the riot gun. Sherman balanced its deadly length on the rail through the port. He snatched at the trigger and his long hand convulsed. The riot gun leaped and chattered.

A white path crashed through the water toward the cockpit of the speedboat. The tall one fell on his face, the gunners pitched over. The pilot of the boat spun the wheel back and forth and pulled down on the throttle. But the white path slashed up to the boat again. Splinters jumped from the thwarts. And, though the boat was hurtling toward shore, the pilot was dead over his wheel.

Sherman stepped back and calmly replaced the clip in the

31

riot gun. Between clenched teeth he said, "I hope they'll appreciate my little message!"

The mate was wiping at the blood over his eye where a splinter had nicked him. "Hell, those fellows mean business!"

Sherman nodded and watched the point intently. He expected to see white mushrooms of smoke issue from those field guns at any moment.

Down on the deck the men in the scuppers were buzzing with excitement. They glanced wonderingly at the man on the bridge, whose marksmanship had been so deadly. They were keyed up, waiting breathlessly for action.

Action was not long in coming. A noise resembling the roar of a freight train came to them, grew louder and louder. A shell from the point landed a hundred yards on the other side of the ship, sending up a green and white geyser of spray. Two thousand yards away, on the end of the arm that enclosed the small harbor, white smoke drifted skyward. White smoke shot up again, and another screaming shell landed near the *Bonito*.

The mate was worried and rushed to the speaking tubes to call the engine room. The words that came back to him were written on his face. It was plain that the reduction gear could not be replaced for some time.

A half hour of the shelling had scored only two minor hits on the *Bonito* and the battery fell silent.

"Now!" cried Sherman. "Here they come!"

Black dots leaped out from the barely visible stone quays, suddenly detached from the green wall of vegetation on the beach. The dots grew in size, and the air was filled with a roar of motors. Four speedboats were bearing down upon the anchored yacht. But they were wary, and circled out four hundred yards from the *Bonito*. Then, with throttled engines, they bobbed around the yacht in a circle.

Sherman motioned to the mate that he could blow his whistle. The shrill blast piped up the men from the scuppers, and sixteen rifles jutted over the gunwale of the *Bonito*.

So far, the fight was in their favor. While shooting from those bobbing speedboats was comparatively inaccurate, the yacht rolled very little, making a steady rest for the rifles of the crew.

Placing the snout of the riot gun through a port in the wing, Sherman sighted a boat and fired a burst. He saw one of the Death Island men pitch over a gunwale into the sea. Sighting again, he pulled the trigger. Then, methodically, he began firing bursts of three and five alternately.

The rifles on deck were beginning to take toll as the men recovered from their first wave of excitement and buckled down to the business at hand. Machine-gun bullets cracked and whined against the *Bonito*'s hull.

Then the second phase of the attack struck from the skies. The battery on the point had their range down to a hair and the air became filled with an almost continuous scream of heavy shells.

With this coming from above them, and machine-gun bullets coming from in front of them, the men of the *Bonito* moved nervously along the rail, cringing each time a shell screamed.

Sherman turned the riot gun over to the mate and went

down on deck. He found Percy Gilman cowering beneath a hatch. With a mighty heave, Sherman brought the fellow to his feet, thrust a rifle into his shaking hands, and threw the quivering figure toward the rail. Bushby was next, and suffered the same fate.

One of the men had fallen, and Sherman picked up his rifle. Going along the rail, he patted shoulders and stepped into a breach here and there, from where he sent a telling shot at the hovering speedboats. In his wake, the men were heartened, and hope flared up.

Sherman completed the rounds of the deck and grasped the bottom of the bridge ladder. The air was suddenly split apart by a rushing shell. There was a heavy, crumpling sound, and a muffled explosion that knocked Sherman back to the planking. Looking up, he saw that the flying bridge was a twisted mass of wreckage. Two of the men had been struck down by splinters, and the chief mate was undoubtedly dead.

Working through and over the wreckage, Sherman came to the platform that had been the bridge. Twisted pieces of brass and wood were all that remained. The dead chief mate was there, his riot gun smashed to bits.

As Sherman ran down the ladder, a shell crashed into the stern, making the entire yacht shudder. A glance back showed that half the crew had been wiped out.

The second mate, Gilman, and Bushby were on their feet with five sailors. All were terribly shaken. But their rifles pumped steadily at the boats that still hovered near.

Sherman turned his back upon the port side, and Gilman

sank quivering to the deck, his face green with fear. Sherman knew that the end was in sight. In less than half an hour the islanders would rush the yacht, swarm up over the sides, and take them all prisoner. He shuddered to think of what would happen to Phyllis Marmion.

Methodically, he began the task of picking off the machine gunners in the speedboats. At four hundred yards, in spite of the mirage caused by water, Sherman's fire was accurate and deadly.

Shells still roared over and crashed about them, sending an occasional splinter of lead screaming over their heads. Bullets ripped and tore into the rails and hull. The second mate was dead, and two sailors were wounded. Bushby and Gilman were nowhere to be seen.

The lead speedboat dashed out of place toward the point and circled twice. The battery became silent. Sherman tensed. He saw that all four boats had begun to run in toward the *Bonito*. It was more than twenty against four.

The first boat came in under the wrecked stern, out of sight of the deck. The second swerved into the protection of the bow. The other two lashed back and forth along the sides, pouring lead into the yacht.

Sherman knew that it would be impossible to keep men from swinging up the anchor chains and up the dragging ropes aft. It was only a question of seconds before he would be flanked on deck. But his fire into the boats did not slacken.

The air was alive with lead. Sherman suddenly saw that he alone was on his feet. The machine guns in the speedboats were suddenly silent. A revolver cracked from the fo'c's'le head.

He snatched the automatic from his pocket and dropped behind a bitt. Men were coming down the forward ladder. Slugs whispered and cracked above him from this new source. He aimed and fired. The first man dropped. He fired again. With only seven shots in all, Sherman was making every one count.

He knew that he was exposed from the rear. Above him, from the wreckage of the bridge, he heard a pistol bark. The sound came again. Glancing up, he beheld a strange figure. Wrapped in a black robe, Phyllis Marmion was taking care of those who would cut down on him from the stern. He saw her wince as the pistol spat again.

Directly in front of him a black face bobbed up on the other side of the narrow bitt. A knife glittered. Sherman shot—but the face was immediately replaced by another.

Then a muzzle pressed into his side and his gun clicked on an empty chamber. Strong arms bore him to the deck. Silence reigned over the battered *Bonito*.

CHAPTER FIVE

BLACK DUNGEONS

ONE by one, those who remained alive on the *Bonito* were brought to the forward deck and lined up against a bulkhead. Sherman was pinned back by two strong natives. Phyllis Marmion stood disdainfully aloof, her black robe wrapped tightly about her. Mr. Marmion clutched at his wife as though for protection. Agnes Loch and Martha Prentice, friends of Mrs. Marmion, cowered before the display of death and arms. Percy Gilman and Edward Bushby were yanked from the fo'c's'le, where they had hidden. And Captain Stoddard sat with his back against the bulkhead, staring dazedly at the proceedings. The chief engineer and his two men made a dark huddle in the shadow of the rail.

A burly mestizo appeared to be the leader of the Death Island men, for he strode back and forth, cracking out commands and rubbing thick hands together as he gazed at his captives.

The leader stepped up to Sherman. "You, again? Ah, but it will be a pleasure this time!" He laughed and jerked a thumb at Phyllis. "Yes, a double pleasure!"

Sherman's answer was flat and calm.

The mestizo gave Phyllis a startled glance, and then crossed himself hurriedly. He bowed slightly, his face serious and reverent. He strode away to give orders to his men.

"What did you tell him?" Phyllis whispered.

One by one, those who remained alive on the Bonito *were brought to the forward deck and lined up against a bulkhead. Sherman was pinned back by two strong natives.*

"Told him you were a nun, so act the part."

Soon they were in the speedboats, whipping in to shore.

They approached two gray stone quays and saw that the town consisted of a crumbling fortress and many yellow and brown houses. All the buildings sat below the fort, backed by a mass of thick tropical vegetation.

It was all an old story to Bob Sherman. He knew their destination and their ultimate fate. This tawdry picture of blue and yellow and green would be their prison.

Cobblestones were under their feet, and people stood in doorways to jeer at them. Mestizo girls, black women, Spaniards and Indians, shouted insults at the group of *Americanos,* told them of their fate in no uncertain terms, and called all the devils and saints to curse them.

As they went up the hill to the fort, Sherman was glad that none of the women spoke Spanish, for the insults had been spoken in the vilest of words.

One by one those from the *Bonito* were thrust through a black postern in the side of the fort wall. Sherman was last in line, but as his guards thrust him forward, he stopped and deliberately turned around. The captors tugged at his arms and then stayed still.

From his place on the hill beside this ruined huddle of masonry, Sherman could see the multicolored roofs of the town below him. He saw the green of the harbor sweeping away into the intense blue of the gulf, saw it meet the sky far out on the Caribbean. The deserted *Bonito* listed tiredly at her moorings. Palms whispered and bent beneath the hot wind.

Then he saw familiar masts, and drew in his breath sharply.

The *Seafarer* lay where he had seen her last, anchored far up the curving beach. From there he swept his eyes back over the scene, noticed the fleecy clouds drifting across the deep blue of the tropical sky from which came the rays of a brassy sun.

He turned and, bending his head low on his chest, entered the postern.

Ahead of him the burly leader bulked dimly in the half-light. His huge arm was holding open a wrought-iron door.

"For old time's sake, you go in here, eh?" He motioned toward the interior of a dungeon. "Remember the happy days you have already spent here, no?"

Sherman stooped and went through the door, down a familiar stone flight of filthy steps, felt decayed straw beneath his feet. He looked back up at the door and saw them shut and lock it.

From the slit of light that came from a small port high on the wall, he could see his own initials carved into the stone wall of the place. A helpless feeling dropped over him, as he remembered the weary hours he had spent carving those letters to keep sane.

Other things were familiar, too. Those rusted wrist and leg irons pinned into the stone. At least they would not put those on him this time. Sherman kicked at them absently, and the iron stabbed through the soggy thinness of his tennis shoes.

The sheer meanness of fate swept up over him, with the dank, decayed odor of the wet stones and straw. He had escaped once and had killed a man to gain his freedom. They would see to it now that nothing like that occurred. Perhaps they planned something a little more strenuous than mere captivity, for Sherman knew that these men of Death Island were past masters in the art of slow torture.

He slumped down with his back to a damp wall and stared at his hands. They were black with grease and powder grime, and here and there a broken blister gaped whitely against the black. Feeling his jaw, he found that the unshaven stubble was stiff against the hardness of his face. His clothes were in rags, clinging to him only by a few strained tatters of grayish duck. The shirt was torn half from his chest, laying bare an expanse of brown skin over rippling muscles.

He wondered where they had placed Phyllis Marmion. She had been next in line to him, and he reasoned that she might be in the next cell. He wondered if his ruse of calling her a nun would protect her. Surely these Spaniards had a deep reverence for their church. All Spaniards had.

He sat up straight and looked along the wall, suddenly remembering an almost forgotten plan of escape conceived nearly two years before. He had hoped to find one of the flanking dungeons unlocked, and to this end he had loosened flat stones in the floor and tunneled through on each side. The tunnels had each succeeded in effecting an entrance to the other cells, but he had found them securely bolted. After that, he had attempted to tunnel under the main wall of the fort, but the foundation was many feet deep and almost as wide. Perhaps those old tunnels were still here and intact.

Excitedly he tapped the stones along the wall. Then,

41

somewhat amazed at the thrill the thought of seeing Phyllis brought, he found the keystone. Pushing at it, he uncovered enough space to allow his fingers a purchase. At the expense of a broken fingernail, he brought the flat stone up and pulled it to one side. Below him gaped that hole he had excavated long ago.

He was just lowering himself into it when the footsteps of a pacing guard made him hurriedly replace the stone. After all, it would be better to wait until darkness fell.

And so he waited.

The sudden dark of the tropics plunged down from the slit and the dungeon became a box of night. Sherman pulled up the stone, finding that his fingers shook. It came away with a dull, rasping sound. He felt below, met the under side of the wall with his fingers. Then he dropped down, moved along and felt stone above his head. Pushing his back up against it, he felt it move up and over from its place. His hands were on the floor of the adjacent cell.

"Phyllis!"

A glum voice answered. It was Bushby.

"Whoever you are, she's not here. They put her two cells up the line. Who is it?"

"You wouldn't be interested." The stone rasped into place and Sherman wriggled back into his own cell. His heart was pounding heavily. Phyllis was on the *other* side of him!

The work of finding the other stone in the dark was not easy, and Sherman wore his fingers to the quick testing the blocks.

Again he felt something give under his impatient hands. The stone came up, slid aside. With his strong back, he lifted the stone above him, felt the cell's flooring under his palms.

"Phyllis!" Hope was vibrant in his whisper.

"Bob!" Phyllis' voice came startled and a little loud.

"Sh! You'll bring the guards. Are you all right?"

Hands were fumbling along the wall, coming closer to him. Something touched his rumpled hair and then passed down around his shoulders aiding him through into the dungeon.

He repeated his question. "Are you all right?"

But her head was buried in his shoulder and muffled sobs took the place of words. In the dark he could sense her misery. Somehow he felt guilty for bringing her into this. He stroked her hair.

Finally she gained control of herself. "Mother is over there in the corner. She's been unconscious with fear most of the day. Can't we do something, Bob? Anything?"

"No, Phyllis. I've tried before."

"But why are they keeping us here? Who *are* these people?"

Sherman sat down along the wall and pulled her close to him. Trying to make his whispers reassuring, he said, "We'll get out of here sooner or later. It just takes patience. Something is bound to happen!" He knew that he lied, but he plunged on. "These people are the exiled scum of Venezuela's criminals and politicians. They come from all along the coasts of the Caribbean. They're hidden here, protected by their guns and fighting men, and no government, even if they knew about them, would be very quick to exterminate them. So long as they limit their activities to occasional piracy, they're let alone. You see, this was once an old pirate stronghold in the days of Morgan."

"But why should they attack us, then hold us prisoners?" Phyllis' voice was low now.

"They think we may be worth something in ransom, though that's just an idea of the bandar-log. They will never try to communicate with the outside world. They wanted what loot they could find on the *Bonito*, and they were afraid we might carry news of them back to civilization."

"I didn't think anything like this could exist in a civilized world!" Phyllis was slightly defiant, as though words could suddenly dispel the seeming illusion of imprisonment.

"It's common, Phyllis. The coast of Africa is bristling with such places. Through China and the Philippines there are thousands of strongholds—full, as many as there used to be in the days of real pirates. Perhaps if you knew Venezuelan politics better, you'd understand that these people aren't wholly scum by comparison. Mexico, Central America, the Caribbean—they're all alike."

"Do you think I'll be—safe here?" Phyllis lifted her head from his shoulder, as though she could see him through the heavy darkness. "You said something about nuns."

"Yes, I said you were a nun. All of these men have a spark of religion in them, and that may protect you."

She pressed her head back against his shoulder and they fell silent, cheered by their closeness to each other, though despair lay heavily in their pounding hearts. At last Sherman broke the silence.

"I saw the *Seafarer* today." He was trying hard to assume a conversational tone. "She looks just as good as the day I last saw her. Canvas seemed to be on the booms, so I guess they must be using her."

Hearing no response, he listened intently. Phyllis was breathing heavily. It comforted him to know that he had brought sleep to her.

Dawn was graying in the dungeon when he got softly to his feet to go. He saw that Mrs. Marmion lay in a pitiful apathy, not caring, not even thinking. Her dull eyes watched him slide into the tunnel and pull the stone into place. Phyllis still slept.

Sherman breakfasted from cold rice and a half-cooked fish, thinking of the shock the fare would bring to the palates of the Marmions. After he had eaten, there began a seemingly endless parade of townspeople, who came to stare through the window at him, pointing and laughing among themselves. But he was used to that. It had happened so many times before.

He was startled to find that he could perceive no gap between the escape months before and his recapture. He was appalled at the quickness with which he reassumed the apathy of a caged animal.

He managed to sleep through most of the day, waking only to find that they had placed a bucket of water in his dungeon. He washed in this, turning the water black with the grime of powder. Then feeling clean and refreshed, he waited for night.

Night was long in coming, and it was still dusk when he again removed the stone in the floor that led to Phyllis' cell.

The knowledge that he loved Phyllis Marmion flickered strongly within him, lighting up the despair in his heart.

Stones met his outstretched palms and he pulled up. "Phyllis!"

Only silence came to him. He called again, a note of worry in his voice. No response. Quickly he poked into the corners of the dungeon, kicking the sodden hay out of them. But the dungeon was bleak and damp and empty. Half hopefully he repeated the search. Then it came to him with staggering swiftness. Phyllis had been taken down into the town! She was gone!

The knowledge was like a knife in his heart and he found himself striding up and down the cell, shaken with dread. He searched again, more to move about than from any hope.

Slowly he replaced the stone and returned to his own dungeon.

CHAPTER SIX

THE NUN

DAYS dragged on down a hot path of monotony. An endless succession of dawns had lighted the dungeon, and a never-ceasing sun had sent that slit of light up across the ceiling of the cell until it seemed to Sherman that it must at last wear a path through the dirty stone. The pile of hay which made up his bed became even more rotten from the dampness, bringing twinges of rheumatism to his tall, hard body.

Each afternoon he went through a series of exercises to retain some of his strength, though the steady diet of rice and fish was hardly conducive to muscle building.

He dreamed constantly and always of Phyllis. Each dream ended in an inevitable nightmare, in which he was unable to save her from the men who had captured him. And after each dream he would lie panting in the heat of the dungeon, fully as tired as though he had actually performed the exertions of which he had dreamed.

And still there was no word of Phyllis. Though he might become dulled against the monotony of the dungeon, the loss of Phyllis was as acute an anguish as it had been that first night when he had found that she was gone.

Although he entered it each night, the cell that had held her for such a short time remained empty. These trips caused him grief that was almost physical in its violence, but he was unable to stifle the hope that some night he would find her. He knew that Bushby and perhaps some of the others were in the next cell, but he did not care to see them, for he knew that then he would have to talk with them, and he found he had no heart for that.

He had grown tired of keeping the calendar on the wall when, one morning, his breakfast was interrupted.

He had been poking distastefully through the cold rice which was heaped on a tin plate, when the spoon caught the corner of something foreign to the plate. He swept the rice to the floor and found that he had disclosed a note. His fingers trembled as he pulled the soggy paper open. Even handwriting lay before him and at the bottom of the page was the word *Phyllis*.

Feverishly he read:

Dearest Bob,

I know you have been terribly worried, but up to now I have been powerless to prevent that. Banish all fears for my safety, for I am amply protected by the cloak you gave me that morning aboard the *Bonito*. I am, to all effects, a nun. Though I knew but little of Catholic religious rites, and though I knew no Spanish at the time, I have managed to bluff it through. My scant knowledge of first aid is in my favor, for I am able to cure their minor sicknesses—though I suspect that it is largely faith in me that does it. I would love to see you as you read this, but that cannot be. I live to the north of the town in a house of my own, and no one troubles me. I am going up on the hill now to bless your rice as it is taken to you. I love you, Bob.

Phyllis

Sherman sat staring at the paper for almost an hour. Again and again he read it through, until it seemed to him that his eyes would wear out the page. Waves of relief and happiness flooded over him. He had an impulse to shout and jump up and down.

Phyllis was safe, and protected against these scavengers of Death Island! That was all that mattered. He could endure imprisonment, anything, so long as she was safe.

Each morning after that he searched through his rice, but that note was the first and last. Still, he was satisfied to know that Phyllis was out of these dungeons, living as she should live—at least in a clean house and with decent food.

The monotonous rut was easier to bear with that thought in mind and with the precious note tucked into what remained of his shirt pocket over his left breast.

The expectation of finding another note spurred on the days, and each time when he found his plate bore only rice, his mind jumped ahead to the next morning when more rice would come.

But his next messenger was not calculated to bring ease to his mind.

The black guard, who brought his food into the dungeon behind the cover of an automatic, was followed one morning by the burly mestizo who had been in command of the boarding party on the yacht. He came down the steps and sat on the final one, holding a pistol on Sherman as he did so.

"You think," he began, "we are going to feed you and keep you comfortable here forever, eh?"

Sherman's eyes bored into the mestizo so that he shifted uncomfortably.

"But," the man said, regaining his swagger, "you are wrong. Oh, very, very wrong. The people are getting bored. They want amusement. Well, you will be the chief entertainer for them. Tomorrow you will act for us. I merely thought you would like to know that we are about to amuse ourselves with you." His voice was gloating. "Ah, yes. You will entertain us." With that he went out, and the door clanged shut behind him.

Sherman sat moodily in the far corner of the dungeon. He had no illusions about what the fellow meant by entertaining. These brutes knew only one amusement, and that was another's torture. They would take him down to the square by the wharf, perhaps tie him to a stake—

He had long ago exhausted all plans of escape, and so he reconciled himself to the fate that awaited him below, in the square of the town. Nothing to do but sit and wait, watch the sun creep up the wall, bringing time closer to his last hour.

That they would be lenient he could not hope. He had killed many of their number, and succeeded in escaping once, and now they would revel in the chance to make him pay.

Once down on his luck, there seemed no pause until he had hit bottom. First there had been this trick of Marmion's which had made Sherman wage battle that had terminated in the loss of those valuable oil lands in Venezuela. Next there had come that crazy hope that he might be able to gain the aid of these scavengers of Death Island in upsetting the government. After that, eighteen months of imprisonment and grueling labor underneath a spinning sun. The fight and the escape, leaving his beloved *Seafarer* behind him. What had ever possessed him to think that he stood a chance of outwitting Marmion by joining the *Bonito* in the guise of a sailor?

The only bright spot in the whole chain of circumstances was the knowledge that he had met Phyllis Marmion. For the second time, perhaps, but then this time had kindled something within him which he knew would never die. He wondered if she would be there to watch his execution. He hoped not. It would be bad enough to be mutilated before the hawk eyes of the outcasts, without having to bear up under her pitying gaze. He didn't want pity from her. He wanted to fight for her, release her from this terrible exile far from her homeland.

He wondered if Bushby and that Percy Gilman and the rest would suffer a like fate. He thought not. They would be kept here until they were sufficiently cowed, then they would be employed at work, degrading work, in the village. Their soft hands would know the burning handles of shovels, and their unprotected heads would bleach under the blast of the tropical sun, just as his own had been bleached.

He felt it now and found that it was matted and tangled. He was filthy and tattered. Well, it was almost better to die by torture than to lose one's mind and self-respect slowly in the half-light of a dungeon.

Night settled at last, and with each dragging hour Bob Sherman's spirits sank lower. There could be no reprieve here.

There was no law to save him at the last moment. Dully he remembered the times in his life he had cursed the existing laws, thinking that they bound him down with wordy chains. But, ironically now, he saw that there could be no civilized world without law—there could be only these mad strongholds of cruelty, where the whim of the moment, the fierce, savage whim was supreme.

His thoughts were stilled by a dull thump made by some heavy object dropping on the floor of his dungeon. Sherman froze, expecting the sound to be repeated. But only the silence of rock, tempered by a faraway pounding of waves came to him. Cautiously he slid along the floor, groping, not knowing what he would find.

Minutes flicked by as he inspected each separate block of stone. Then at last his fingers encountered a hard, rough object the size of his fist. Holding it up he found that a string was attached to it. Following down the string, he clutched at a slip of paper.

He knew that it was a note, probably from Phyllis. But the blackness of the dungeon mocked at him, holding its opaque curtain between his eyes and the writing he knew to be there.

Sitting hunched over the note he waited impatiently for dawn, which would bring the light he needed. They were long, terrible hours of waiting, but at least they kept his mind from dwelling upon the fate the day was about to mete out to him.

Grayness probed through the slit, making the wisps of straw glow dimly on the stone. Sherman stood on tiptoe below the window, holding the unfolded paper to the light.

GET 4 FREE BOOKS!

You can have the titles in the Stories from the Golden Age delivered to your door by signing up for the book club. Start today, and we'll send you **4 FREE BOOKS** (worth $39.80) as your reward.

───○►───

The collection includes 80 volumes (book or audio) by master storyteller L. Ron Hubbard in the genres of science fiction, fantasy, mystery, adventure and western, originally penned for the pulp magazines of the 1930s and '40s.

───○►───

YES! ☑

Sign me up for the Stories from the Golden Age Book Club and send me my first book for $9.95 with my **4 FREE BOOKS** (FREE shipping). I will pay only $9.95 each month for the subsequent titles in the series. Shipping is FREE and I can cancel any time I want to.

First Name _____ Middle Name _____ Last Name _____

Address _____

City _____ State _____ ZIP _____

Telephone _____ E-mail _____

Credit/Debit Card #: _____

Card ID# (last 3 or 4 digits): _____ Exp Date: _____/_____

Date (month/day/year) _____/_____/_____

Signature: _____

Comments: _____

Thank you!

Bob dearest,
Do not worry. I love you.
Phyllis

He whipped at the paper and then read it again. No, there were no other words. What did she mean? What could she possibly do to help him? Perhaps she was merely trying to ease the last few hours for him. One girl against all the people of Death Island? Impossible!

Sherman found himself walking back and forth over his cell, his steps quick and catlike. He had only those few words to hearten him, though he was positive that any plan she might conceive would be cut down before it could get under weigh. Then he began to fear for her safety. If she was caught in any attempt to liberate him, her fate, whether she was considered a nun or not, would be sealed.

Surely she had no weapon mighty enough to hold all Death Island at bay. That she was brave enough to try she had already proven aboard the *Bonito,* when her pistol had kept them from shooting him down from behind.

And so the hours of the morning passed and gave place to the slanting rays of the afternoon sun against the roof of the dungeon. Sherman watched the slit with bated breath. Footfalls would come to him soon, and Spaniards and mestizos would drag him away to that cobblestone square in front of the quays, to lash him beneath the pitiless sun, to mutilate his strong body.

At last the footsteps came, rough and without rhythm, up the passageway. They came with voices raised in hilarity. It was plain that this was to be a gala occasion for *la isla de la muerte.*

The dark mestizo kicked the door wide, stood in the threshold, his thick hands on his fat hips. Faces jutted over his shoulders, staring down into the dungeon.

CHAPTER SEVEN

DEATH BY TORTURE

SHERMAN stood in the center of the floor and looked up. Then he walked calmly to the stairs and reached the door. Heavy hands closed about his arms, thrusting him ahead. He made no resistance and looked neither to the right nor left.

The postern opened before him and strong sunlight smote his unaccustomed eyes. Blinded to the colorful scene spreading before him, he felt the rough path under his feet.

When his sight returned, they were on the cobblestone street of the town. The quays were before him, backed by the green of the harbor. Colored dresses in the doors of the houses swung into line behind him as he was pushed on. Voices had become an unceasing roar in his ears.

As he entered the square before the quays, he saw that the *Bonito* was gone, probably sunk, against prying eyes. But the *Seafarer* lay far up the beach, her masts bare, swinging gently in the offshore breeze.

Beside the quays were the four speedboats, machine guns mounted in the bows, pointing toward shore. Sherman noted that the boats were empty and quickly weighed his chances of getting to one of them. But already they were swirling about him. He saw ropes in brown hands, saw that he was facing a tall stake in the center of the square.

They twisted him about, his back almost flat to the huge stake. People were a mass of shifting, noisy color in front of him, to each side of him.

He thought of Phyllis and decided that the note had merely been intended to cheer up that long night. It had been kind of her to do that. She was probably locked securely in her house to the north of town.

Sherman was glad that she hadn't been able to do anything, endangering her own life. Perhaps she would be able to get away later. He was glad, too, that she was not in the crowd about him. It would have made it too hard to die.

The burly mestizo came close to him and laughed. With his thick arms he swept the crowd away from the stake. With slow fingers he finished tying Sherman securely, so that he could not move.

Sherman was almost as tall as the stake, towering above the surrounding crowd. His tattered clothing did not rob him of a certain dignity which he bore in his aloofness. Now and then the breeze tossed his blond hair down into his eyes. Where his shirt was ripped open, the sun beat in hotly upon him.

The mestizo held a thin case of knives in his hands, holding them up for all to see. They were the surgeon's knives Sherman had always kept aboard the *Seafarer,* and their thin blades were as keen as light. The burly one flipped up the cover and laid the case on the cobblestones at Sherman's feet. Carefully selecting a lancet he stood up and drew back his lips, showing wide, tobacco-stained teeth.

The crowd opened in front of Sherman and a little native hurried forward to the mestizo, shouting loudly as he came.

"The nun!" he cried. "She is gone!"

"*¡Por Dios! ¡Ave Maria!*" shouted the mestizo. "You were her guard!" Snatching the little native up by his shirtfront, the mestizo raised the lancet. Sunlight snapped from the blade as it came down.

Sherman's eyes narrowed and his mouth thinned as he watched life ebb from the writhing wretch on the cobblestones. Rivulets of that life were collecting in pools among the stones.

The mestizo stood up straight, looked about the circle with indecision, and turned back to Sherman.

"No matter. She can't go far. We'll attend to that later," he said.

With a vicious blow, the mestizo snapped Sherman's blond head back. The lancet came down lightly across the throat. Sherman felt its sting, then felt blood running down into his shirt. His tormentor laughed, and the crowd roared in echo.

Sherman knew that this would keep up for hours. The next slash would not be in fun.

The mestizo had changed the lancet for a scapula.

The gaudy crowd suddenly hushed as all eyes followed the scapula. But the scapula never reached its destination.

A sharp, chattering clatter bit through the air. Men and women on Sherman's left were falling sidewise, scrambling along the cobblestones. The crackle stopped, then began again. It seemed to come from the harbor.

The crowd at Bob's right pitched into sudden activity,

swirled down to the cobblestones, staggered or ran toward the houses. The people in front of the stake whirled and ran up the street. The mestizo darted to one side, clutched at his hairy chest, brought his fingers away red.

Sherman stood transfixed. Something seared his arm and he hugged it tight to his side. He saw that he alone was left upright in the square.

Two men kicked open the shutters of a house, and rifles were thrust out toward the harbor. The shrill clatter came again, and two bodies pitched through the opening to the cobblestones. Then, momentarily, there was silence.

By straining his foot forward from the stake, Sherman found that he could touch the reddened lancet with his toes. By rubbing its heel against the wood, he removed the ragged tennis shoe and reached forward again. There was barely a chance that he could bring the knife up within reach of his hand.

His toes closed over the small hilt, bringing the lancet away. Sherman bent his knee carefully, straining to one side. He forced his shin back into the stake and thrust his arm down until he could touch his ankle. With a wrench he snatched down at the lancet, felt its keen blade bite into his fingers.

It was only a moment's work to twist the lancet about until it cut the rope. The hemp slithered away from him. He broke away from the post and hesitated an instant, looking toward the quays. One of the speedboats which lay closest in to the square had its machine gun leveled in the bows. A ray of sunlight fell on a thick mass of black hair. A white arm shot up from the thwarts, waving to him to come on.

With a glad cry, Sherman sprinted across the fifty feet of cobblestones that intervened.

"Phyllis!" He was beside the boat.

"Get down! They'll start shooting any second!" Her eyes flamed with excitement. "Lordy, Bob, I thought this thing never would start shooting! It was all I could do to get it loaded. You better put a new belt in."

Sherman grinned and slid out, until he lay at full length behind the cowl. He patted her shoulder and snatched a new belt from the bottom of the boat. After he had placed the belt through the feed box and cocked the gun ready for action, he felt about for the motor's starter.

Less than a minute later the boat's engine roared alive. Sherman put the gears into reverse and they scudded back from the quay. With the gears in neutral, he took the gun's handle from Phyllis. Bullets began to whisper about them and pit the water.

The hulls and stems of the other three boats snapped into the sights, and Sherman pressed the trips. Splinters jumped ahead of him and round holes appeared just above the waterlines of the other crafts.

"That's good enough!" Phyllis cried. "Let's head for the *Seafarer*!"

The speedboat spun about and rushed along the beach, slashing a white streak along the face of the water. They crouched in the protection of the gunwale, raising up now and then to see that the *Seafarer* was growing larger ahead.

"She's all set," Phyllis shouted above the roar of the engine. "I swam out last night."

Sherman placed his mouth close to her ear. "How did you think of this?"

She pointed to a tangle of canvas under the after thwarts. "Hid under that since dawn. Worried to death for fear I wouldn't be able to load and fire this machine gun."

He jerked up straight and spun the wheel. They sped under the overhang stem of the *Seafarer* and came up along the port side, protected from shore by the yacht. With the painter of the speedboat in his hand, Sherman slid up to the deck and pulled the girl after him.

Aside from a thick coating of dirt, the schooner yacht was just as he left her. Tangles of loose gear showed that she had been used.

Stripping a halyard from a belaying pin, Sherman called the girl to him.

"You'll have to give me a hand with the sails."

Together they pulled and the light gaff leaped up the mast in a flutter of wind-whipped canvas. Bullets snapped into the gunwales and sang off the bitts, but the jibs cracked up.

Phyllis raced down the deck to the wheel, while Sherman spun a miniature capstan, raising the anchor. As the beach began to swing past the sprit, Sherman saw that several small boats were putting out to them.

Water was boiling under the stem as he took the wheel. Ahead lay the Caribbean and the mouth of the gulf. Canvas had ceased to snap and now bellied full as the brisk wind drove the yacht out to sea.

With the beach thousands of yards behind them, and the

battery of field guns outranged, Phyllis perched herself on the top of the after cabins above the binnacle.

"Lordy, Bob, but it's a treat just to look at you!" She smiled and Sherman saw that the tropical sun had tanned her skin, giving her face a warm touch of color.

She continued, "We'll go get a couple navies and go back after the others."

"No, Phyllis. No navies would listen to us. We'll wait until dark and tackle them again."

Phyllis looked at his determined mouth, started to speak, and then shrugged.

"Okay, sir. You're captain of this packet. I don't know how we'll do it, but, then, you can do anything."

"You're the genius of this family," he laughed. "It took real nerve to play the hand you played this afternoon."

"But if it hadn't been for you, and my confidence in you, I'd never have been able to tackle it. So," she spread out her hands expressively, "we're even."

Rolling waves of the Caribbean were under the plunging bow of the *Seafarer*, and Death Island receded to a speck in the far distance. Sherman drew in great lungfuls of the clean salt air.

"You never appreciate freedom until you're caged, do you?" Phyllis sat beside him and pulled the blond head down. Her kiss was frank. "Now! I feel better. You go below and put on some decent clothes, if you can find any. I'll take the wheel. Your throat needs dressing, too."

Sherman stopped in the companionway and looked back at her. The wind was tugging at her white skirt and whipping back the collar of her blouse. Her hair was loose and falling about her shoulders, catching the sun. Her eyes were happy.

The cabins were dirty and dusty from disuse. The table tops were spotted with bottles, and the rugs burned by many careless cigarette butts. Strangely enough, Sherman found that the clothes in his lockers had not been touched. They were complete, even to the evening clothes.

In the mirror over a wash basin he gave himself a wondering look. His cheeks were sunken and white, and his beard was a matted tangle.

A dull razor and some laundry soap were sufficient to remove the offending beard. He used a bottle of rum for tonic and antiseptic for his light wounds. The salt water felt cool and delicious as he bathed his lean body. Clean, fresh underwear felt alien to his skin. Brushing the mold from a pair of blue serge sailor pants, he donned them, securing them with a black belt and heavy brass buckle. A black shirt and a pair of dancing pumps completed his dress.

Pulling a yachting cap over his right eye, he swung back up the companionway and strode to Phyllis, who was at the wheel. He swept her up off her feet and held her before him. Then he brought her close to him and kissed her.

"What ho!" said Phyllis. "A symphony in black. What are you—the Black Terror himself?"

Sherman set her up above the binnacle and took the spinning wheel. He grinned and straightened the *Seafarer* out on her course.

"Black Terror of the Spanish Main," he said. "You've no idea how it feels to wear real clothes again. Those whites were just about rotted off from me. Now tell me all about your experiences."

"Nothing much to tell. I just bluffed my way through as a servant of the church. I hope the church won't cast me out when it hears about it." She smiled down at him. "They brought everything and anything to me to cure, and after I learned how to speak their Spanish, they brought all their confessions. If it weren't so risky, we could go back and blackmail the island to death."

"Seems to me, Phyllis, you did your best to bring about its death this afternoon with that machine gun." He jerked his thumb toward the speedboat they had in tow. "I'll wager you downed no less than fifty of the brutes."

Phyllis shuddered. "Please, let's not talk about it. I hate to think I really killed men."

"Looks like we're going to have a squall." Sherman looked up at fleeting black clouds. "That ought to simplify things a little."

"At least *something* is in our favor."

"You take the wheel, Phyllis. I'm going below to see if the auxiliary engine is in working order. We'll need it to get back to Death Island tonight."

Phyllis saluted. "Aye, aye, Captain."

A half hour later the engine room telegraph beside her rang and shifted its needles. The *Seafarer* began to steer easier.

Sherman came back aft. "There's plenty of gas in her. They

must have gotten it off the *Bonito*. I'll let her run for a while, just to make sure."

Phyllis pulled a handkerchief from her pocket and wiped a smudge from his nose.

"There, now you're all clean again." Her face became serious. "Listen, Bob, even though we do get the rest of them out of there alive and ourselves included, how is this going to help out that oil deal of yours in Venezuela?"

"We'll worry about that later." He took the wheel away from her. "Now we'll head back to Death Island."

With the darkness came a rush of rain and wind, and the blackness lay so heavy about them that they could establish the position of Death Island only by the lights of the town, shimmering now and then through the driving rain. The sea had become rough, and the schooner yacht plunged heavily, fighting her wheel. Now and then a whitecap threw a phosphorescent arc around her bows, making the brimming scuppers glow whitely for an instant.

It was a spectral night, and the spell of it silenced the two aboard the *Seafarer*. It was not until they sighted the first lights of the town that they fully realized the danger of their return. Guards would be out patrolling the beaches and quays, and guns would not long withhold their fire. While an element of surprise was in their favor, it was one thing to land on Death Island, quite another to liberate ten people from a fortress.

They stood close together at the wheel, while the wind shrieked through the rigging above them.

"Where is your mother?" Sherman asked.

"Probably back in the fort by this time. She stayed with me in the hut." In the half-light of the binnacle, Sherman saw that the girl's face was strained. Suddenly she clutched at him. "Oh, Bob! Can't we turn around and sail away? We can get somebody else to come back and get them. I'm so afraid that something terrible will happen again."

He held her close to him, feeling the black hair whip damply against his face. "Don't worry. Luck's turned in our favor now. I think I can do it easily enough."

He went forward, and Phyllis heard the sails slithering down. A motor purred somewhere inside the yacht.

Holding the girl tightly to him for an instant, Sherman slid over the stem and pulled the speedboat up under him. He was almost invisible in his black clothes, and Phyllis was not quite sure when he dropped. The lights of the town shimmered through the crash of the rain and wind.

Sherman pulled an oar from under the thwarts and paddled through pitch blackness toward Death Island. His only hand weapon was a monkey wrench in his hip pocket, and his plan of action had yet to be entirely formulated. . . .

Waves steadied out under the speedboat's keel and Sherman heard the soft rasp of sand beneath him. Bracing his heels in the beach, he pulled the speedboat up, with a prayer that the waves would not take it away.

Wind whipped through the palms, making an eerie, clattering sound. The roar of the surf was an ominous undertone to the sound of the trees. The lights of the town showed blurred through the storm.

Sherman took the heavy wrench from his pocket and hefted

it. With its weight swinging at his side, he plunged into the soaked jungle. Vines tore at his feet and thorn bushes ripped at his arms, but he pounded on toward the fort.

At last he came out into a clearing. He was going uphill, and knew that he must be approaching the fort. With luck he would be able to get to the postern unseen.

The howl and lash of the storm was in his favor, for it meant that guards would be hunched against the rain, their watchfulness weakened by their physical misery.

A rough wall soared up before him. He felt along it, seeing by the fitful gleam of the lights below that he must travel to the right to reach the door. He shifted the wrench and felt his way along, pressed hard against the rocks. He would have to be careful, lest he blunder into the postern unprepared.

Wrought iron was beneath his searching fingers, and the path lay smooth under his feet. Feeling out, he found no one around the door. The wrought iron swung back and he was inside, out of the rain. Far ahead a lantern flickered under the gusts that moaned through the fort. Pressed back against the side of the passage, Sherman inched forward, his light shoes silent. Aside from his face, he was a black shadow against the blackness of the entrance.

The unsuspecting guard nodded in back of the lantern. Sherman was beside him when the guard looked up and snatched at the rifle across his knees. The fingers barely touched the butt before they twitched and spread slowly out. Sherman brought the wrench back to his side and pulled the body over against the wall. He started on up the corridor.

A shout rang out behind him. Before he could whirl, the passage echoed with the roar of a pistol shot. Sherman swooped down and picked up the guard's body, holding it in front of him. The passage was filled with other roars, and the body in Bob's hands twitched from the impact of slugs as he carried it steadily forward.

The burly mestizo was barely outlined by the lantern light as he stood trying to miss the guard and shoot Sherman. The mestizo saw the body suddenly leap for him, and dodged. The dodge was fatal, for before he could cry out again, steel fingers closed on his throat.

Sherman let the mestizo slump to the floor and picked up the automatic. It was empty, and he cast it aside. Ripping at the clothing of the mestizo, Sherman found the keys.

Closing and locking the postern, he picked up the lantern and went to the first cell. Disheveled figures sat up, and dull eyes blinked at the light. It was the chief engineer and his two sailors.

"Come out!" Sherman snapped. "There's no time to lose. Those pistol shots may have been heard in the village!"

Silently the three rushed to the door where the chief engineer found the guard's rifle. Then, with a grim expression on his Scotch face, he went down to the postern.

Bushby and Gilman babbled incoherently, almost faint with excitement as they scrambled up out of their dungeon. Captain Stoddard dazedly followed them, stumbling weakly. The three stood in an indecisive huddle against the corridor.

Sherman found Mr. Marmion and his wife together. The

realization that they might soon be free was almost too much for them, and Mr. Marmion's desperate fingers twisted at Sherman's sleeve.

Sherman told them to go down to the end of the passage. He then turned to the last cell.

Huddled together, almost out of the lantern's radius, Martha Prentice and Agnes Loch clung together miserably.

"Go away, do you hear? Go away!" one cried wretchedly.

Sherman leaped down over the stone steps and pulled them both from the floor with one motion.

"Come quickly! We haven't got much time—you're free!"

The two still clung together, tugging their rags about them. They clung together anew when they saw the dead men in the passage, but Sherman hurried them on down to the postern.

He counted noses and found that he had all ten. Then the chief engineer thrust the postern open, and, holding hands to prevent any of them from getting lost, they went on up along the wall, Sherman leading the way, the engineer bringing up the rear.

As they slid down the hill toward the jungle, a shout arose behind them. Someone had found the dead mestizo and guard in the passage. With this to lend new speed to their weakened legs, the ten scurried on through the stormy blackness. Other shouts were answering the first.

Then the jungle was ripping at them, tripping them up, surrounding them with its mysterious noises and rain.

Sherman thrust them back, with an admonition for silence, and called the chief engineer up beside him.

"Listen," he whispered, "I'm not sure where the speedboat is. You keep up a sharp lookout while I find it." He crept silently away across the soft sand.

Waves on the shifting beach were under his feet, lapping about his ankles. The palm trees moaned and rattled above him, as though they themselves were the skeletons of Death Island. The surf roared in his ears as he made his way along.

Then something hard cracked into his shin, making him wince, and he knew that he was beside the speedboat. Waves reached his knees, and he started to feel his way up toward the bow, when a sudden icy hand clutched at him. Two men were seated silently on the beached craft, waiting at the bow for him to return. He had only evaded instant discovery by walking in the water, hitting the boat near the stem.

He hefted the monkey wrench and drew a deep breath. If he missed, that was that. Something shiny loomed up ahead. That was the machine gun. A shadow was beside it, at the handles, waiting for a target.

The wrench thumped into something that yielded sharply. A startled exclamation from the bow followed. With no other course, Sherman threw himself toward other shadows, the wrench heavy in his hand.

Things were tearing at him, but the wrench found its mark. Taken by surprise, the Death Island men went down.

Sherman stood up, breathing heavily—but he had counted his victory too soon. A shrill cry split through the roaring night, and the sound of departing feet went away from the speedboat. Without pausing, Sherman raced back to the waiting ten.

He shouted, and heard the engineer shout back. Feet, pitiful, faltering feet, were coming to him over the sand. Shadows loomed around him, and he led the way back to the speedboat, quickly helping each one over the gunwale into the craft. He heard one of the older women gasp, and knew that she had touched the man who had lain in wait behind the machine gun.

The chief engineer and the two sailors were standing by at the gunwales, ready to push the craft out from the beach. Sherman gave the word, and sand began to grate under the keel. The air was tense about him, for he knew that, even now, men might be creeping up on them from the jungle.

That shout had carried far even in this wind-lashed blackness.

But the boat was rocking on the waves before a cry was raised ashore. The cry was quickly followed by running and several stabs of flame. The chief engineer slid under the wheel and the motor roared alive.

"Duck! Everybody down in the bottom!" Sherman leaped to the machine gun. "I'm going to fire over your heads."

The belt felt soggy under his hand, but he pressed the trigger and a roar answered him. The gun writhed up and down on its mount, sending a hail of lead from the flaming muzzle. Flashes were answering, furnishing targets for his hammering weapon.

The speedboat roared away from the beach, hurtling over the waves, skimming one, dropping into a trough of the next. The lights of the town faded rapidly.

Sherman knew that the roaring whine of the motor could be heard even above the thunder of the night, and he directed the engineer to head for the spot where he had left the *Seafarer,* counting upon the motor to give Phyllis the knowledge that they were coming.

And the motor's roar was enough. When they were a half mile from the beach, a clear shaft of brilliance shot high up into the air. Phyllis had found the yacht's searchlights.

The engineer bore straight as an arrow down the yellow shaft. The yacht's side loomed above them and the speedboat curved around, coming up against a lowered gangway.

Martha Prentice and Agnes Loch went shakily up, followed by the other eight. Sherman held the speedboat's lashing length against the landing stage until the last one had disappeared over the rail. Then he passed up the painter and drifted the boat aft.

The auxiliary motor was throbbing below, and the engineer showed that he knew something of sail by raising the gaffs, with the help of his sailors. The *Seafarer's* bows were crashing into the waves as she bore her rescued cargo far out into the Caribbean.

Sherman found Phyllis at the wheel, and gathered her close in his arms.

With her head buried in his wet shoulder, she said, "Oh, but I've been in agony ever since the second you dropped off the stern!"

One of the sailors came aft and Sherman told him the course, waving him to the wheel. Then he picked Phyllis up in his arms and took her down the companionway to the cabins. He looked down at the wet black hair which streamed water on the rug, and saw a smile light up her face.

Marmion was a tattered scarecrow perched on a leather transom. Others of the group had found their way to staterooms. Phyllis threw her arms about her father's neck and kissed his worry-ravaged face.

"Oh, Dad!" she cried. "I'm so glad to see you alive! We'll never be able to thank Bob Sherman for what he's done for us!"

In spite of the happenings of the night and his joy at seeing his daughter again, at the sound of the name Sherman, Phyllis' father sat up straight.

"Sherman! Is this the Bob Sherman—?"

"Yes," Sherman said. "This is the Bob Sherman you took the oil lands away from. And before we go any further, I want you to turn all those oil lands over to Phyllis."

Marmion blinked and sat back. "But—but—how will that help you? I know I owe them to you, after all this, but how can that do you any good?"

Phyllis got up and stood beside Sherman, looking up at him as he put an arm about her.

Marmion got to his feet and shook hands with Sherman. "So that's the way it is! Well, I'm not surprised. Looks as though I'll lose both oil land and Phyllis."

"Do you mind, Dad?"

"Well—" Marmion hesitated. "No," he said then. "Not in the circumstances. It's a sort of poetic justice."

Phyllis flashed him a radiant smile and turned to Sherman. Her father faded out.

He isn't so bad, is he, Bob?" she said.

"Being your father—" Sherman smiled and drew her close. "Love me, Phyllis?"

Phyllis' eyes danced. "Must I answer that?" she whispered, and with her lips against his, no other answer was needed.

STORY PREVIEW

NOW that you've just ventured through one of the captivating tales in the Stories from the Golden Age collection by L. Ron Hubbard, turn the page and enjoy a preview of *The Phantom Patrol*. Join Officer Johnny Trescott on a deadly sea adventure when a drug runner captures his Coast Guard boat, and uses it and Johnny's uniform to raid ships and traffic drugs. When authorities arrest Johnny and throw him in jail, he must escape and bring the cutthroat to justice—or face the gallows himself.

THE PHANTOM PATROL

F RIENDS of yours?" asked Mac.

Johnny whirled. Through the tumble of water he could see a vague shape drawing abreast of them. It was a black low-lying cruiser of ominous proportions.

"Get below!" rapped Johnny at the two pilots and the girl.

When they had gone, Heinie held on tight and stared at the ship, which was drawing nearer. "Who is it?"

"Three guesses, Heinie. The first three don't count."

"My God, Johnny! You mean that's Georges Coquelin?"

"In person. Run up some shells for the one-pounder and have Haines break out a machine gun. We're going to have a little party."

"But they're too close! They'll blow us out of the—" A towering sea battered Heinie against the side of the deckhouse. He struggled toward the hatch.

Johnny gave the black ship a bitter smile. No one knew better than he that the presence of Georges Coquelin was not a coincidence. That line in the SOS about Ferguson . . . Ferguson could be held for ransom—big ransom.

"Run out the shells!" bawled Johnny after his retreating exec. "We'll hold him as long as we can." He thumped the holstered .45 which banged against his thigh.

The pitching black line cruiser began to slacken

speed. Its wake still boiling, it swerved around in a three-hundred-and-sixty-degree turn to come back alongside. A tall blond man was holding the bridge rail with tight fists. Two sailors worked at something shiny behind the wheel. A machine gun.

Johnny lurched toward the deckhouse. Inside he grabbed the brass tube. "Joe! Get going! Georges sneaked up on us. Full speed!"

"Hell!" bellowed Joe, deep in the ship. "We strained a reduction gear while we were laying to!"

"Did you take it apart?"

"Yes."

"Why, of all the—! Okay, Joe. If you don't get it together in five minutes, you won't have any engines to monkey with. Snap into it!"

Heinie struggled up to the dripping one-pounder with a box of shells which he jammed into the rack. Johnny slued the weapon about.

A smooth voice drifted across the intervening hundred yards. "Lay off that gun, sailor. We want Ferguson."

The megaphone rolled in the scuppers. Johnny snatched it up. "Go to hell!" he shouted.

From the bridge of the pitching black ship came a sound like a thousand hammers beating simultaneously on tin. A window shattered in the deckhouse. Slugs ripped splinters from the planks.

Johnny rammed a shell into the breech. He waited until the patrol boat bucked upward. The lanyard jerked and the gun jumped. Heinie slammed another into the breech.

"Lower!" bawled Heinie. "Hull him! Don't try for the bridge!"

A sailor came up beside Johnny. "I'll take it."

Johnny stepped aside and picked up the megaphone. The machine gun had stopped.

"Coquelin! Shove off, or we'll sink you!"

The tall blond man on the cruiser's bridge threw back his head and laughed. Then he shouted through cupped hands, "Look at my forward deck!"

The black ship was drawing astern of them. The patrol boat was pitching in the trough, hard to hit and harder to shoot from. On the forward deck of the cruiser, a three-inch gun was menacing them. Beside it a one-pounder was a child's plaything.

"Knock the pants off him," begged Heinie. "He's not so tough. We'll run away from him in a minute."

"The hell we will. That dumb son Joe dismantled the reduction gear while we were taking the people off the plane."

The gray sky met the green sea. The waves smashed and roared over the forward deck. The black ship was astern and coming up on the starboard side. The range was less than fifty yards, but a dozen frowning mountain ranges intervened. The blond man on the bridge gripped the rail and leaned forward expectantly. Behind him two men crouched beside the machine gun, waiting for his signal.

Johnny fought his way back to the deckhouse. "Joe!" he shouted into the tube. "Can't you *do* something?"

"In a few minutes, Johnny—"

"Step on it. There aren't many left!"

Back on deck, Johnny heard Coquelin shout, "Lay off that gun or I'll blast you. Hand over Ferguson."

Johnny turned to Heinie. Past Heinie, the sea was waltzing through thirty degrees. The patrol boat's bucking made it hard to stick with her.

"He means it," said Johnny. "It won't be the first time. Hold your fire with that gun, sailor. We couldn't get him the first shot."

"What you going to do," raved Heinie, "stand there and let him take Ferguson? We'd be the laughing stock of the base! For God's sake, Johnny!"

"Shut up. We've got passengers aboard us and I've got to protect them, haven't I?"

Georges Coquelin loomed more distinct as the distance lessened between them. He was Johnny's height and had Johnny's blond hair and leathery complexion. "What about it?" He pointed significantly at the three-incher. Sailors were peeling off the canvas lashings and making ready with a shell.

Out of the patrol boat's after hatch, a sailor struggled up with a machine gun.

"Hold that fire!" shouted Johnny.

"We can't fight," Heinie wailed. "The devil's got the drop on us. If we just—" They were buried again in the green swirl. When the wave had gone, the pitching black ship was still there. The wind screamed through the radio mast of the CG-1004.

On the black ship's bow were the words *The Maid from Hell.*

To find out more about *The Phantom Patrol* and how you can obtain your copy, go to www.goldenagestories.com.

GLOSSARY

GLOSSARY

STORIES FROM THE GOLDEN AGE *reflect the words and expressions used in the 1930s and 1940s, adding unique flavor and authenticity to the tales. While a character's speech may often reflect regional origins, it also can convey attitudes common in the day. So that readers can better grasp such cultural and historical terms, uncommon words or expressions of the era, the following glossary has been provided.*

---

astern: in a position behind a specified vessel.

bandar-log: a term used in Rudyard Kipling's *The Jungle Book* to describe monkeys. In Hindi, *bandar* means "monkey" and *log* means "people."

bandoliers: broad belts worn over the shoulder by soldiers and having a number of small loops or pockets, for holding cartridges.

belay: stop.

belaying pin: a large wooden or metal pin that fits into a hole in a rail on a ship or boat, and to which a rope can be fastened.

binnacle: a built-in housing for a ship's compass.

bitt: a vertical post, usually one of a pair, set on the deck of a ship and used for securing cables, lines for towing, etc.

black gang: ship's crew that works in the engine room aboard a ship. They were called *black* because of the soot and coal dust that was thick in the air in the fire room/engine room.

Black Terror: a reference to Sir Henry Morgan (1635?–1688), known as the King of the Buccaneers and terror of the Spanish Main. Morgan was one of the most ruthless of pirates; his daring, brutality and intelligence made him the most feared, and respected, buccaneer by his friends and enemies alike.

capstan: a device used on a ship that consists of an upright, rotatable cylinder around which ropes, chains or cables are wound, either by hand or machine, for hoisting anchors, lifting weights, etc.

Cartagena: a seaport in northern Colombia.

*Coast Pilot*s: official publications giving descriptions of particular sections of coast and usually sailing directions for coastal navigation.

fathom: a unit of length equal to six feet, used in measuring the depth of water.

field pieces: mounted guns; cannon.

flying bridge: a small, often open deck or platform above the pilothouse or main cabin, having duplicate controls and navigational equipment.

fo'c's'le: forecastle; the upper deck of a sailing ship, forward of the foremast.

gaff: a pole rising aft from a mast to support the top of a sail.

gangway: a narrow, movable platform or ramp forming a bridge by which to board or leave a ship.

G-men: government men; agents of the Federal Bureau of Investigation.

gunwale: the upper edge of the side of a boat. Originally a gunwale was a platform where guns were mounted, and was designed to accommodate the additional stresses imposed by the artillery being used.

halyard: a rope used for raising and lowering a sail.

keel: a lengthwise structure along the base of a ship, and in some vessels extended downwards as a ridge to increase stability.

lanyard: a cord attached to a cannon's trigger mechanism which, when pulled, fires the cannon.

Lucas reel: the brand name of a machine used for sounding or measuring the depth of an area of water.

mestizos: people of racially mixed ancestry, especially in Latin America, of mixed American Indian and European, usually Spanish or Portuguese, ancestry.

Morgan: Sir Henry Morgan (1635?–1688), a Welsh buccaneer in the Americas. His brutal hostilities against the Spanish colonies in the Caribbean are known for their skillful execution, at times, against great odds. An exaggerated account of his exploits, written by one of his crew, created his popular reputation as a bloodthirsty pirate.

one-pound gun or **one-pounder:** a gun firing a one-pound shot or shell. It looks somewhat like a miniature cannon.

packet: packet-boat; originally a vessel that carried mail, passengers and goods regularly on a fixed route.

painter: a rope, usually at the bow, for fastening a boat to a ship, stake, etc.

pink tea: formal tea, reception or other social gathering usually attended by politicians, military officials and the like.

Point Gallinas: a cape in northeastern Colombia at the northernmost point of South America.

por Dios: (Spanish) for God's sake.

postern: a small gate or entrance at the back of a building, especially a castle or a fort.

reduction gear: a set of gears in an engine used to reduce output speed relative to that of the engine while providing greater turning power.

scapula: a surgical knife with a broad wedge-shaped cutting edge.

Scheherazade: the female narrator of *The Arabian Nights,* who during one thousand and one adventurous nights saved her life by entertaining her husband, the king, with stories.

schooner: a fast sailing ship with at least two masts and with sails set lengthwise.

scuppers: openings in the side of a ship at deck level that allow water to run off.

sea anchor: a device, such as a conical canvas bag, that is thrown overboard and dragged behind a ship to control its speed or heading.

ship's articles: the contract containing all particulars relating to the terms of agreement between the captain of the vessel and a crew member in respect to wages, length of time for which they are sailing, etc., signed prior to and upon termination of a voyage.

sprit: bowsprit; a spar projecting from the upper end of the bow of a sailing vessel, for holding and supporting a sail.

stem: the forwardmost part of the bow.

stern: the rear end of a ship or boat.

telegraph: an apparatus, usually mechanical, for transmitting and receiving orders between the bridge of a ship and the engine room or some other part of the engineering department.

thwart: a seat across a boat, especially one used by a rower.

transom: transom seat; a kind of bench seat, usually with a locker or drawers underneath.

under weigh: in motion; underway.

weigh anchor: take up the anchor when ready to sail.

well deck: the space on the main deck of a ship lying at a lower level between the bridge and either a raised forward deck or a raised deck at the stern, which usually has cabins underneath.

L. Ron Hubbard
in the Golden Age
of Pulp Fiction

*In writing an adventure story
a writer has to know that he is adventuring
for a lot of people who cannot.
The writer has to take them here and there
about the globe and show them
excitement and love and realism.
As long as that writer is living the part of an
adventurer when he is hammering
the keys, he is succeeding with his story.*

*Adventuring is a state of mind.
If you adventure through life, you have a
good chance to be a success on paper.*

*Adventure doesn't mean globe-trotting,
exactly, and it doesn't mean great deeds.
Adventuring is like art.
You have to live it to make it real.*

—*L. RON HUBBARD*

L. Ron Hubbard
and American
Pulp Fiction

B ORN March 13, 1911, L. Ron Hubbard lived a life at
least as expansive as the stories with which he enthralled
a hundred million readers through a fifty-year career.

Originally hailing from Tilden, Nebraska, he spent his
formative years in a classically rugged Montana, replete with
the cowpunchers, lawmen and desperadoes who would later
people his Wild West adventures. And lest anyone imagine
those adventures were drawn from vicarious experience, he
was not only breaking broncs at a tender age, he was also
among the few whites ever admitted into Blackfoot society
as a bona fide blood brother. While if only to round out an
otherwise rough and tumble youth, his mother was that rarity
of her time—a thoroughly educated woman—who introduced
her son to the classics of Occidental literature even before
his seventh birthday.

But as any dedicated L. Ron Hubbard reader will attest, his
world extended far beyond Montana. In point of fact, and as the
son of a United States naval officer, by the age of eighteen he
had traveled over a quarter of a million miles. Included therein
were three Pacific crossings to a then still mysterious Asia, where
he ran with the likes of Her British Majesty's agent-in-place

L. Ron Hubbard, left, at Congressional Airport, Washington, DC, 1931, with members of George Washington University flying club.

for North China, and the last in the line of Royal Magicians from the court of Kublai Khan. For the record, L. Ron Hubbard was also among the first Westerners to gain admittance to forbidden Tibetan monasteries below Manchuria, and his photographs of China's Great Wall long graced American geography texts.

Upon his return to the United States and a hasty completion of his interrupted high school education, the young Ron Hubbard entered George Washington University. There, as fans of his aerial adventures may have heard, he earned his wings as a pioneering barnstormer at the dawn of American aviation. He also earned a place in free-flight record books for the longest sustained flight above Chicago. Moreover, as a roving reporter for *Sportsman Pilot* (featuring his first professionally penned articles), he further helped inspire a generation of pilots who would take America to world airpower.

Immediately beyond his sophomore year, Ron embarked on the first of his famed ethnological expeditions, initially to then untrammeled Caribbean shores (descriptions of which would later fill a whole series of West Indies mystery-thrillers). That the Puerto Rican interior would also figure into the future of Ron Hubbard stories was likewise no accident. For in addition to cultural studies of the island, a 1932–33

LRH expedition is rightly remembered as conducting the first complete mineralogical survey of a Puerto Rico under United States jurisdiction.

There was many another adventure along this vein: As a lifetime member of the famed Explorers Club, L. Ron Hubbard charted North Pacific waters with the first shipboard radio direction finder, and so pioneered a long-range navigation system universally employed until the late twentieth century. While not to put too fine an edge on it, he also held a rare Master Mariner's license to pilot any vessel, of any tonnage in any ocean.

Yet lest we stray too far afield, there is an LRH note at this juncture in his saga, and it reads in part:

"I started out writing for the pulps, writing the best I knew, writing for every mag on the stands, slanting as well as I could."

To which one might add: His earliest submissions date from the summer of 1934, and included tales drawn from true-to-life Asian adventures, with characters roughly modeled on British/American intelligence operatives he had known in Shanghai. His early Westerns were similarly peppered with details drawn from personal experience. Although therein lay a first hard lesson from the often cruel world of the pulps. His first Westerns were soundly rejected as lacking the authenticity of a Max Brand yarn

Capt. L. Ron Hubbard in Ketchikan, Alaska, 1940, on his Alaskan Radio Experimental Expedition, the first of three voyages conducted under the Explorers Club flag.

(a particularly frustrating comment given L. Ron Hubbard's Westerns came straight from his Montana homeland, while Max Brand was a mediocre New York poet named Frederick Schiller Faust, who turned out implausible six-shooter tales from the terrace of an Italian villa).

Nevertheless, and needless to say, L. Ron Hubbard persevered and soon earned a reputation as among the most publishable names in pulp fiction, with a ninety percent placement rate of first-draft manuscripts. He was also among the most prolific, averaging between seventy and a hundred thousand words a month. Hence the rumors that L. Ron Hubbard had redesigned a typewriter for faster keyboard action and pounded out manuscripts on a continuous roll of butcher paper to save the precious seconds it took to insert a single sheet of paper into manual typewriters of the day.

That all L. Ron Hubbard stories did not run beneath said byline is yet another aspect of pulp fiction lore. That is, as publishers periodically rejected manuscripts from top-drawer authors if only to avoid paying top dollar, L. Ron Hubbard and company just as frequently replied with submissions under various pseudonyms. In Ron's case, the

---

A MAN OF MANY NAMES

Between 1934 and 1950, L. Ron Hubbard authored more than fifteen million words of fiction in more than two hundred classic publications. To supply his fans and editors with stories across an array of genres and pulp titles, he adopted fifteen pseudonyms in addition to his already renowned L. Ron Hubbard byline.

Winchester Remington Colt
Lt. Jonathan Daly
Capt. Charles Gordon
Capt. L. Ron Hubbard
Bernard Hubbel
Michael Keith
Rene Lafayette
Legionnaire 148
Legionnaire 14830
Ken Martin
Scott Morgan
Lt. Scott Morgan
Kurt von Rachen
Barry Randolph
Capt. Humbert Reynolds

list included: Rene Lafayette, Captain Charles Gordon, Lt. Scott Morgan and the notorious Kurt von Rachen—supposedly on the lam for a murder rap, while hammering out two-fisted prose in Argentina. The point: While L. Ron Hubbard as Ken Martin spun stories of Southeast Asian intrigue, LRH as Barry Randolph authored tales of

L. Ron Hubbard, circa 1930, at the outset of a literary career that would finally span half a century.

romance on the Western range—which, stretching between a dozen genres is how he came to stand among the two hundred elite authors providing close to a million tales through the glory days of American Pulp Fiction.

In evidence of exactly that, by 1936 L. Ron Hubbard was literally leading pulp fiction's elite as president of New York's American Fiction Guild. Members included a veritable pulp hall of fame: Lester "Doc Savage" Dent, Walter "The Shadow" Gibson, and the legendary Dashiell Hammett—to cite but a few.

Also in evidence of just where L. Ron Hubbard stood within his first two years on the American pulp circuit: By the spring of 1937, he was ensconced in Hollywood, adopting a Caribbean thriller for Columbia Pictures, remembered today as *The Secret of Treasure Island*. Comprising fifteen thirty-minute episodes, the L. Ron Hubbard screenplay led to the most profitable matinée serial in Hollywood history. In accord with Hollywood culture, he was thereafter continually called upon

95

The 1937 Secret of Treasure Island, *a fifteen-episode serial adapted for the screen by L. Ron Hubbard from his novel,* Murder at Pirate Castle.

to rewrite/doctor scripts—most famously for long-time friend and fellow adventurer Clark Gable.

In the interim—and herein lies another distinctive chapter of the L. Ron Hubbard story—he continually worked to open Pulp Kingdom gates to up-and-coming authors. Or, for that matter, anyone who wished to write. It was a fairly unconventional stance, as markets were already thin and competition razor sharp. But the fact remains, it was an L. Ron Hubbard hallmark that he vehemently lobbied on behalf of young authors—regularly supplying instructional articles to trade journals, guest-lecturing to short story classes at George Washington University and Harvard, and even founding his own creative writing competition. It was established in 1940, dubbed the Golden Pen, and guaranteed winners both New York representation and publication in *Argosy*.

But it was John W. Campbell Jr.'s *Astounding Science Fiction* that finally proved the most memorable LRH vehicle. While every fan of L. Ron Hubbard's galactic epics undoubtedly knows the story, it nonetheless bears repeating: By late 1938, the pulp publishing magnate of Street & Smith was determined to revamp *Astounding Science Fiction* for broader readership. In particular, senior editorial director F. Orlin Tremaine called for stories with a stronger *human element*. When acting editor John W. Campbell balked, preferring his spaceship-driven tales, Tremaine enlisted Hubbard. Hubbard, in turn, replied with the genre's first truly *character-driven* works, wherein heroes are pitted not against bug-eyed monsters but the mystery and majesty of deep space itself—and thus was launched the Golden Age of Science Fiction.

The names alone are enough to quicken the pulse of any science fiction aficionado, including LRH friend and protégé, Robert Heinlein, Isaac Asimov, A. E. van Vogt and Ray Bradbury. Moreover, when coupled with LRH stories of fantasy, we further come to what's rightly been described as the foundation of every modern tale of horror: L. Ron Hubbard's immortal *Fear.* It was rightly proclaimed by Stephen King as one of the very few works to genuinely warrant that overworked term "classic"—as in: *"This is a classic tale of creeping, surreal menace and horror. . . . This is one of the really, really good ones."*

To accommodate the greater body of L. Ron Hubbard fantasies, Street & Smith inaugurated *Unknown*—a classic pulp if there ever was one, and wherein readers were soon thrilling to the likes of *Typewriter in the Sky* and *Slaves of Sleep* of which Frederik Pohl would declare: *"There are bits and pieces from Ron's work that became part of the language in ways that very few other writers managed."*

And, indeed, at J. W. Campbell Jr.'s insistence, Ron was regularly drawing on themes from the Arabian Nights and

L. Ron Hubbard, 1948, among fellow science fiction luminaries at the World Science Fiction Convention in Toronto.

so introducing readers to a world of genies, jinn, Aladdin and Sinbad—all of which, of course, continue to float through cultural mythology to this day.

At least as influential in terms of post-apocalypse stories was L. Ron Hubbard's 1940 *Final Blackout*. Generally acclaimed as the finest anti-war novel of the decade and among the ten best works of the genre ever authored—here, too, was a tale that would live on in ways few other writers imagined.

Portland, Oregon, 1943; L. Ron Hubbard, captain of the US Navy subchaser PC 815.

Hence, the later Robert Heinlein verdict: "Final Blackout *is as perfect a piece of science fiction as has ever been written.*"

Like many another who both lived and wrote American pulp adventure, the war proved a tragic end to Ron's sojourn in the pulps. He served with distinction in four theaters and was highly decorated for commanding corvettes in the North Pacific. He was also grievously wounded in combat, lost many a close friend and colleague and thus resolved to say farewell to pulp fiction and devote himself to what it had supported these many years—namely, his serious research.

But in no way was the LRH literary saga at an end, for as he wrote some thirty years later, in 1980:

"Recently there came a period when I had little to do. This was novel in a life so crammed with busy years, and I decided to amuse myself by writing a novel that was pure *science fiction."*

That work was *Battlefield Earth: A Saga of the Year 3000*. It was an immediate *New York Times* bestseller and, in fact, the first international science fiction blockbuster in decades. It was not, however, L. Ron Hubbard's magnum opus, as that distinction is generally reserved for his next and final work: The 1.2 million word *Mission Earth*.

> **Final Blackout**
> *is as perfect a piece of science fiction as has ever been written.*
>
> —Robert Heinlein

How he managed those 1.2 million words in just over twelve months is yet another piece of the L. Ron Hubbard legend. But the fact remains, he did indeed author a ten-volume *dekalogy* that lives in publishing history for the fact that each and every volume of the series was also a *New York Times* bestseller.

Moreover, as subsequent generations discovered L. Ron Hubbard through republished works and novelizations of his screenplays, the mere fact of his name on a cover signaled an international bestseller. . . . Until, to date, sales of his works exceed hundreds of millions, and he otherwise remains among the most enduring and widely read authors in literary history. Although as a final word on the tales of L. Ron Hubbard, perhaps it's enough to simply reiterate what editors told readers in the glory days of American Pulp Fiction:

He writes the way he does, brothers, because he's been there, seen it and done it!

THE STORIES FROM THE GOLDEN AGE

Your ticket to adventure starts here with the Stories from
the Golden Age collection by master storyteller L. Ron Hubbard.
These gripping tales are set in a kaleidoscope of exotic locales and brim
with fascinating characters, including some of the
most vile villains, dangerous dames and brazen heroes
you'll ever get to meet.

The entire collection of over one hundred and fifty stories is being
released in a series of eighty books and audiobooks.
For an up-to-date listing of available titles,
go to www.goldenagestories.com.

AIR ADVENTURE

FAR-FLUNG ADVENTURE

SEA ADVENTURE

TALES FROM THE ORIENT

The Devil—With Wings *Pearl Pirate*
The Falcon Killer *The Red Dragon*
Five Mex for a Million *Spy Killer*
Golden Hell *Tah*
The Green God *The Trail of the Red Diamonds*
Hurricane's Roar *Wind–Gone–Mad*
Inky Odds *Yellow Loot*
Orders Is Orders

MYSTERY

The Blow Torch Murder *The Grease Spot*
Brass Keys to Murder *Killer Ape*
Calling Squad Cars! *Killer's Law*
The Carnival of Death *The Mad Dog Murder*
The Chee-Chalker *Mouthpiece*
Dead Men Kill *Murder Afloat*
The Death Flyer *The Slickers*
Flame City *They Killed Him Dead*

FANTASY

SCIENCE FICTION

WESTERN

The Baron of Coyote River
Blood on His Spurs
Boss of the Lazy B
Branded Outlaw
Cattle King for a Day
Come and Get It
Death Waits at Sundown
Devil's Manhunt
The Ghost Town Gun-Ghost
Gun Boss of Tumbleweed
Gunman!
Gunman's Tally
The Gunner from Gehenna
Hoss Tamer
Johnny, the Town Tamer
King of the Gunmen
The Magic Quirt

Man for Breakfast
The No-Gun Gunhawk
The No-Gun Man
The Ranch That No One Would Buy
Reign of the Gila Monster
Ride 'Em, Cowboy
Ruin at Rio Piedras
Shadows from Boot Hill
Silent Pards
Six-Gun Caballero
Stacked Bullets
Stranger in Town
Tinhorn's Daughter
The Toughest Ranger
Under the Diehard Brand
Vengeance Is Mine!
When Gilhooly Was in Flower

JOIN THE PULP REVIVAL
America in the 1930s and 40s

Pulp fiction was in its heyday and 30 million readers were regularly riveted by the larger-than-life tales of master storyteller L. Ron Hubbard. For this was pulp fiction's golden age, when the writing was raw and every page packed a walloping punch.

That magic can now be yours. An evocative world of nefarious villains, exotic intrigues, courageous heroes and heroines—a world that today's cinema has barely tapped for tales of adventure and swashbucklers.

Enroll today in the Stories from the Golden Age Club and begin receiving your monthly feature edition selected from more than 150 stories in the collection.

You may choose to enjoy them as either a paperback or audiobook for the special membership price of $9.95 each month along with FREE shipping and handling.

CALL TOLL-FREE: 1-877-8GALAXY
(1-877-842-5299) OR GO ONLINE TO
www.goldenagestories.com
AND BECOME PART OF THE PULP REVIVAL!

Prices are set in US dollars only. For non-US residents, please call
1-323-466-7815 for pricing information. Free shipping available for US residents only.

Galaxy Press, 7051 Hollywood Blvd., Suite 200, Hollywood, CA 90028